agency to an enigmatic and fascinating female figure from ancient Hindu lore, while exploring and seeking to resolve the proverbial and vexing tension between asceticism and sensuality'

Prof Philip Lutgendorf

'Engaging and cinematic narrative'

Srijit Mukherjee

'A stream of consciousness; a spiritual telling. It rescued and redeemed the purity ruse. Koral is a visual writer'

Nabila Jamshed

'A stunning read. Fluent and engaging. What a fine writer!'

Fiona Sampson

'Panchakanya and other women, reinterpreted, is a most pertinent call. *Ahalya* is beautifully written and the little details and imagined conversations bring the character alive. I also enjoyed the almost surrealistic movement between mythical time and ours. It's a reminder that we in India live by a philosophy of transitions, an in-between-ness. Ahalya is amongst us'

Prof Malashri Lal

'Powerful ... The novelty of the novel lies in the fact that no other writer has talked about Ahalya vis-à-vis her womanhood'

Outlook

'In a most intriguing retelling, Dasgupta's narrative turns the seduction story on its head, making Ahalya the seducer instead of the seduced'

Scroll.in

'An ecocritical reading of *Ahalya* reveals the exploration of an ancient connection with nature that's sacred, intimate, and as we are in the midst of an environmental emergency, vital to reconcile with today'

Firstpost

'[T]he brilliance of Dasgupta's retelling is not just within the confines of that transformation itself, but rather, the importance of being seen, validated and loved as you are'

Southern Humanities Review

'Koral Dasgupta creates true wonder with her new book *Ahalya*'

Tempest

'A stunning piece of literature'

Dipannita Sharma

Praise for *Kunti*

'Koral Dasgupta writes about Kunti, one of the Pancha Kanyas, with verve, emotion and passion. Her highly readable account of this fascinating character, who played a key role in the Mahabharata, is a must for those wishing to know about our past and the dialectics of gender within it'

Pavan K. Varma

'Koral Dasgupta makes the ancient myths speak in new and unexpected voices; voices that have been lost and sunken in the dominant narrative consciousness, and yet, the voices of characters who made the flesh, blood and the values of the epics possible'

Saikat Majumdar

Advance Praise for *Tara*

'Embedded within the epic saga of the Ramayan, *Tara*'s nuanced narrative is bathed in grace and empathy. We enter the non-textual world of the vanaras to discover a deep worldview through the voice of an extraordinary protagonist'

Namita Gokhale

'A powerful depiction of Tara's world, encompassing Bali and Sugreev, with distinct ideologies influencing the rules of the Kishkindha kingdom'

Amish

'Exuberant and imaginative, this narrative about kinship, friendship and love explores questions about borders: between the animal and the human, the wild and the tame, the living and the dead, the revelatory and the remembered, heaven and earth, language and silence. With a cast of vividly etched characters and a feel for the mysteries that lie at the heart of intimacy, here is a fascinating tale by an inventive and thoughtful storyteller'

Arundhathi Subramaniam

Praise for *Ahalya*

'Ahalya, Draupadi, Kunti, Tara, Mandodari – each of the Pancha Kanyas is fascinating. Ahalya's story has been told and retold several times, sometimes with varying accounts across texts. What was her relationship with Gautam and Indra? What was her crime? How was she redeemed? Why is she among the Pancha Kanyas?

There have been modern retellings and interpretations too. Koral Dasgupta's wonderful retelling adds to this corpus, with a lyrical and poetic quality. The image that will remain with you is of the Mist ... Enthralling'

Bibek Debroy

'"Go, woman, find your world yourself. The joy you seek deserves to be discovered." Armed with this advice, Ahalya sets off on her life's journey. The magical and thought-provoking adventure that follows will intrigue and mesmerize readers'

Chitra Banerjee Divakaruni

'Koral Dasgupta's evocation of Ahalya, the first of the Pancha Kanyas, the five virtuous women from Indian myth, is an enigmatic tale about purity, chastity, seduction and redemption, told from the perspective of the eternal feminine'

Namita Gokhale

'Amazing premise and approach. This is one unique take on an age-old tale. Brilliant and intriguing'

Anand Neelakantan

'Impressed. I literally never imagined the interior world of a character from mythology in this way, let alone contemplating this way of reflecting on the soul, embodiment, desire and a woman's experience of the Brahma- and Indra-dominated worlds! Really powerful'

Prof Brian A. Hatcher

'In this original and spirited interpretation of the tale of Ahalya, Koral Dasgupta gives voice, character and

'Bringing heroines of yore, like Ahalya and Kunti, to contemporary times, Koral Dasgupta writes with a rare verve and energy. Never dull or pedantic, she makes the woman within the legend come alive. A rare talent'

Makarand R. Paranjape

Praise for *Draupadi*

'*Draupadi* lives up to the expectations set by *Ahalya* and *Kunti* ... Koral [Dasgupta] dares to boldly push the narrative in ways you cannot imagine. A must-read'

Kiran Manral

'This is a striking rewriting of Draupadi's story. Koral Dasgupta has given us a Draupadi who is fearless, politically astute and unwilling to be anyone's victim. This Draupadi leans into her power and changes the course of history in Dasgupta's beautifully crafted world'

Prof Tracy Pintchman

'In poetic prose Koral Dasgupta weaves surprising threads into the ever-evolving tapestry of the Mahabharata, enriching it with this empowering, lyrical telling of Draupadi's life'

Prof Hillary P. Rodrigues

'Koral Dasgupta has given us a unique take on a well-known story from the Mahabharata. It is fascinating to hear this tale from a female perspective, to hear

[Draupadi's] thoughts and struggles about being offered in marriage to all five brothers, as well as her eventual realization of the purpose behind the marriage. This work clearly shows Draupadi to be an intelligent and rational player in the divine plan. In our attempts to make the academic world more diverse and accessible to all, a reading of Draupadi alongside the Mahabharata would be an excellent way to open new dialogues in the classroom and beyond'

Prof Arnold Smit

'This lyrical and insightful reimagining of Draupadī's narrative is a worthy entry in the long tradition of telling the tales of India's (and the world's) great epics'

Prof Brian Collins

'A lively series of beloved stories from ancient India that speak to modern readers'

Prof Paul B. Courtright

Praise for *Mandodari*

'Imaginative, intense and insightful ... Narrated in Koral's signature style, the exchanges of Mandodari and Sita (and their implications for Ravan and Ram) are absolutely fascinating'

Ashwin Sanghi

'[*Mandodari*] has several strengths, including, but not limited to, Dasgupta's envisioning of the inner world of the women of Lanka, the differences, sympathies and alliances within, as well as the titular character's moral turbulence'

Telegraph

'*Mandodari* with its lyrical prose and philosophical moorings ... conjures up visions of a mesmerizing world. The book shows how so much is made possible by a lone woman's resilience and unswerving commitment to do the right thing'

New Indian Express

TARA

KORAL DASGUPTA has published an eclectic range of books, from academic non-fiction to relationship dramas. Her books are discussed in the context of gender studies, art, myth and ecocritical literature. Other than India, Koral's books can be found in the libraries of Harvard University, Columbia University, the University of Pennsylvania, University of Chicago, University of Wales, Duke University, University of North Carolina, Texas A&M University, among others. The books in the Sati series have been nominated for various prestigious awards, with *Ahalya* most recently being recommended for the 2023 Sahitya Akademi Prize Honour List.

Koral is the founder of www.tellmeyourstory.biz and conducts writing programmes and critical thinking workshops for educational and corporate floors. She has been recognized on the Innovator25 Asia Pacific 2019 list prepared by the Holmes Report and featured in the Women of Wonder (WOW) series in *Outlook Business* magazine.

Her website is www.koraldasgupta.com.

Also in the Sati series

Ahalya

Kunti

Draupadi

Mandodari

TARA

KORAL DASGUPTA

THE SATI SERIES V

PAN

First published 2024 by Pan
An imprint of Pan Macmillan Publishing India Private Limited
707 Kailash Building
26 K. G. Marg, New Delhi 110001
www.panmacmillan.co.in

Pan Macmillan, The Smithson, 6 Briset Street, Farringdon, London EC1M 5NR
Associated companies throughout the world
www.panmacmillan.com

ISBN 978-81-19300-75-4

1 3 5 7 9 8 6 4 2

Typeset in Guardi LT Std by R. Ajith Kumar, New Delhi
Printed and bound in India by Thomson Press India Ltd.

MIX
Paper | Supporting responsible forestry
FSC® C116313
FSC www.fsc.org

For my son, Neev Tanish

CONTENTS

SERIES INTRODUCTION

The Pancha Kanyas of Hindu mythology are Ahalya, Kunti, Draupadi, Mandodari and Tara, while the five Satis include Sita, Sati, Savitri, Damayanti and Arundhati. The distinction between these two different titles arose primarily because certain versions of the epics have taken the liberty to celebrate women as per the popular beliefs of their era and, of course, those of the translators. One school of thought defines 'Sati' as symbolizing the women's unconditional devotion to and dependence on their men. It casts the women as loyal followers, strongly supporting the vision of the men around them or helping them overcome social and emotional challenges. These women are depicted as self-sacrificing and selfless, yet invincible when drafting their own position of strength and authority.

Various senior scholars translate the Pancha Kanyas as 'five virgins'. Thus, based on textual evidence, the Kanyas and Satis are different women. However, in the earliest texts, there is no mention of the Pancha Satis; they only talk about the Pancha Kanyas who are deemed as the Maha Satis. Even in regional interpretations, especially in some eastern and southern states of the country, this division is blurred. This could be due to the difference in the spread of the Mahabharat of Vedavyasa versus the dissemination of Valmiki Ramayan. The former specifically mentions the Pancha Kanyas.

Many versions of the Ramayan discuss the Satis in terms of loyalty and physical chastity. Such women, including Sita, aren't restricted to only five. But they don't club them under the umbrella term, Pancha Sati. In my own studies, I came across some scholarly assumptions that the

Satis were reborn as Kanyas, with research trying to draw parallels!

An ancient *shloka* establishes that reciting the names of the Pancha Kanya can dispel sins, which again confirms the 'Sati' status of these women. Sati, meaning pure, devoted and fair. Purity that cannot be destroyed by external influence, because criticism or judgment cannot deflect one from her chosen path of righteousness.

In the Sati series, I follow this conception of 'purity' while retelling the stories of the five illustrious women: Ahalya, Kunti, Draupadi, Mandodari and Tara. The purity that is brave enough to present itself the way it is – sans any cosmetic cover – and mirrors the mind unpretentiously as much as it exposes the politics of a society.

However, the Sati series is not meant to be biographical. The purpose of the series is to draw attention to a part of the journeys of these legendary women that have been grossly overlooked. Identities have been imposed based on incidents that the patriarchy considered criminal, shameful or irresponsible. When these known events adopt the narrative voice of a feminine titular character, the stories change. The world expands. The Sati series not only presents an inclusive overview of the protagonist's own life but also dives deep into the suppressed pain of those around them – be it a man or a woman.

In the first, fourth and fifth book of the series, *Ahalya, Mandodari* and *Tara,* the entire narrative had to be recreated. About Kunti and Draupadi, a lot is known already. My retellings spotlight the making of these characters, albeit from a non-traditional perspective, which ushers the readers into a new era of thinking and reimagining.

Ahalya introduced the woman as a lover. Ambitious, futuristic, royal and calculative; not afraid to express, nor hesitant to ignore the binding rules of the world. *Kunti* called for a relook at the patriarchal origins of 'Mata' and, in relation, the pervasive sociopolitical image of the sacrificing Indian mother. *Draupadi* was even more complicated than the previous books because it shed light on the societal reactions across generations towards crimes against women, particularly those who are successful. *Mandodari* sparked yet another powerful discourse on the critical choices faced by an accomplished woman between the calls of of her mind and heart, in light of a terrible sin committed by her extremely talented husband. *Tara,* the last book of the series, brings up the discourse of human–animal politics, highlighting the grandeur of certain traditions of the forest and the wisdom of animals that transcends boundaries. It also explores the sensitivity that prompts a woman to forgo the blinds borne by the diplomatic crown of a queen.

Ram's killing of Bali while hiding behind a bush is a disturbing episode from the Ramayan that I personally could never digest. Tara's narrative opens with an acknowledgement of Bali's death and then travels through the sequence of events – securing some emotional and logical derivatives.

PROLOGUE

Queen Mandodari,

As I write this letter, I wonder whether my words will reach you. We, the animals, express ourselves in more ways than one, but a script is the first of its kind. I believe it will further communication, especially in interpersonal and diplomatic relationships. Initially, we will need interpreters, such as Hanuman. Later, the curve will slope, and language will flow.

Sugreev encouraged my attempts; Bali was not amused.

'Why do you spend time on something so unimportant?' he would ask, repeatedly climbing up a *tamal* tree and jumping down.

'How is this not important?' I would be taken aback.

'We have a voice and a body. Those are enough for articulation.'

Bali would stroke my face with his tail and tilt his head to the right, revealing a wide range of teeth. It irritated me when he did this.

'A script will transmit crucial messages from one source to another when direct interaction is not possible.' I slapped him on the back with a swing of my tail.

'Why is such transmission required?'

This would make me look up. Bali was watching me innocently. If only he were anything close to innocent ... We kept having these arguments. 'What do you mean? When putting together a kingdom and protecting it from its enemies, the messages will need to discreetly reach the right destination. This will maintain transparency with allies and give you an edge over the opponent.'

He shook his head like a stubborn child. 'When we are attacked, we fight. When we receive love, we love back. Things are simple and straightforward. Writing will complicate matters.'

For Bali, the world was linear, and its rules were meant to be effortless. He didn't see principles changing really fast or virtues being revised.

'Bali, don't speak just because God has given you a mouth. You have been gifted a brain, too. Use it. Talk sense, at least sometimes.'

He relaxed, his body stretching out. 'Persuade me,' he challenged.

'Do you realize that a script could document history? Whatever is happening today, the problems we are facing, the solutions we are coming up with, the stories of our community and vegetation, the land and its practices – all these could serve as a comprehensive reference for the future,' I said with great excitement.

Bali was hardly swayed. 'You really think so?' He sat up restlessly. 'What if the future finds such documentation restrictive? What if historical narratives limit the imagination of upcoming generations? No, wait.' He stopped me as I was about to erupt. 'What will you write about? The making of Kishkindha? How we've stitched a system together?' He did a backflip. 'Think about it. What if this history impels its readers to stop thinking beyond us? What if they immerse themselves in the vanity of something they have not contributed to, and flaunt the glory of ancestors as their own defining identity instead? Every new generation must engrave its independent achievements. Don't let the accomplishments of one era become baggage for another!'

My head was reeling now. Passion is always crazy, ideals are unwavering. One has to spend a day with Bali to endure their extent. He was smiling at my furious face. I don't know whether Bali truly believed what he said or if it was a trick to get me to talk. He hated when I remained silent, withdrawn or thoughtful. From dropping bananas in my vicinity to raising a storm of dry leaves by shaking the surrounding trees, he would attempt all kinds of distractions just to hear me shout, 'Bali, stop!' He would then rush in, sit close to me, brushing his arm against mine.

'You mean history is futile? Keeping a chronological note of events is a stupid occupation?' I asked angrily, picking up a few pebbles from the ground. He chuckled again, displaying his prominent teeth.

'History is not futile; historians are.' He laughed loudly and dodged the stone I had thrown, pointing to his ear. 'Historians politicize events. Preferred characters become heroes; anyone questioning the heroes is vilified. Historians forget to file how many were deceived by the inspirations of an epoch – every great personality hides a trail of undocumented cruelty.' Bali was running now, as I chased him through the mango forest. He picked up a fruit and gobbled it on the run, throwing the peel and the seed at me. 'The human race salutes manipulative writers. May the animals be spared. Aaarrrgh ... slow down, woman,' he groaned, as some pebbles landed on his back. 'What is remembered is all that matters. Only memories are real. Documentation is deceitful.' He disappeared between the tall grasses and towering trees.

I stopped, scanning my surroundings to trace him. He was surely watching from somewhere, yet I couldn't even hear him breathing. Climbing the branches of a tree, I leapt up to survey until the edges of the Pampa Lake. He was nowhere to be seen.

Useless fellow.

I jumped down and turned around. There he was, holding an earthen pot, eyeing me strangely. I charged at him, slapped his head and jabbed his belly, making him fall as I caught the pot of water just before it spilled. Desperately gulping down the liquid, my grip loosened, and the pot crashed to the ground. My victim was rubbing his head where I had struck him.

'Sugreev!'

Bali's twin looked up. 'Are you mad? Bali told me you wanted water to drink,' he accused.

'You believed? How can you fall for his pranks again and again?' I rebuked.

Sugreev didn't answer. Nor did he mention that I, the wife, had been duped by the prank as well. Quietly, he moved on. These two looked terribly alike. Countless times, the elder one had planted mischief, getting the younger one into trouble and leaving everyone else embarrassed.

Oh, Mandodari, I sat down to write a letter to you and see how I've digressed right from the beginning. Even after his death, I am consumed by the thoughts of Bali. They haunt me everywhere, claiming time and attention. It's as if I've just come back from chasing him to converse with you. My heart is still racing as I recall how Bali kept me on my toes. My past and my present, my verity and my hallucination, have merged into a gigantic delusion. Bali has already begun his solitary trek into a larger world. Yet, I remain trapped by my love for him, seeking him as mine, longing and lusting for him, feeling happy for him and getting angry at him.

Mandodari, pardon me for this slip.

I will not scrap the personal episodes I have scribbled down. Let me warn that we, the animals, do not arrange our narratives in a standard sequence like humans. We recount things as they appear to us, whether cordial or cruel. You might have reasons to loathe us, Mandodari. And, you might also feel a certain kinship. Too many common threads have mercilessly entwined both our lives. Your terrific brothers, Dunduvi and Mayavi, had sent shockwaves through the animal kingdom. Bali eventually killed them to protect the forest-dwellers. These killings came at a heavy cost, though, transforming the loving twins into bitter enemies. Dormant demons awakened, leaving one dead and the other burdened with guilt for life. You can understand the pain of death. This is the only plane where all forms of life are unconditionally aligned. Distinctions perish with death. Only crushing regret remains. At this stage in life, where you've lost Ravan, and Bali is a bygone, our chaotic paths have shed their embellishments. You and I have become women who breathe in the present but live in the past, walking hand in hand with invisible mementoes.

My script and Bali's words are both rendered inadequate.

Bali used to speak very highly of Ravan – a terrifying enemy turned dependable friend. He praised the latter's knowledge in body-crafting, astronomy and Ayurveda. I owe you an important story.

Those were the days when Kishkindha had been newly set up. A lot of work remained to make the systems functional. On his way back from the Himalayas, Ravan learnt about this remarkable forest kingdom, ruled by a graceful monkey. Whether he wanted to experience its splendour or destroy the supremacy of the animals, I don't know. Ravan barged into Kishkindha.

Everyone had heard about the Asur king defeating Kuber and ousting him from his own country. Sugreev was frightened. Ravan glared at the quivering *vanjula* flowers beside the Pampa and proposed a war with Bali. At that time, Bali was travelling in the coastal regions of the west, praying to his gods. Ravan left to find Bali, leaving behind a trembling Sugreev in anticipation of tumultuous destruction. Within a few days, however, we woke up to a scene that none of us had expected. Bali and Ravan were returning to Kishkindha, hands on each other's shoulders, chatting and laughing like two long-lost friends had reunited. Bali never told anyone what happened between them, nor did Ravan.

Folk artists seldom miss an opportunity. Their lyrics spoke of an arrogant Ravan discovering Bali on the banks of the Narmada River, deep in meditation. Unwilling to disturb the worshipper, Ravan waited indefinitely for Bali to rise. When the latter did not get up after several days, Ravan grew angry. He tried lifting the huge monkey by his tail. Not even its tip could be displaced. As hard as Ravan tried, the tail seemed to gain weight, mocking the Asur monarch and making him sweat and puff. Bali remained absorbed in his meditation. Feeling insulted and assuming it to be some esoteric trick of the animals, Ravan jumped over the tail, sitting with his legs on either side. He drew his sword to chop the monkey's pride into pieces. The long tail suddenly recoiled, holding Ravan tight within its turns. The sword fell from Ravan's hands. Before he could react, Bali opened his eyes, still chanting his prayers to the river, and took a giant leap. If only Ravan could have guessed what he had got himself into!

After his prayers, it was Bali's ritual to take a round of the world. He paid homage to Mother Earth and the sea. His flight was his liberation, cutting through the air with tremendous speed. Trapped within the twists of his tail, the world whirling around him, and fur entering his nose and ears, the mighty Ravan sneezed and strained. Yet he could not move even a finger. Constricted within the tight coils, his skin developed rashes.

Ravan stopped trying. Gritting his teeth, ears hurting from the rush of wind, hair going haywire and the heart threatening to pop out of its diaphragm, he waited for Bali to return to land, all the while chanting the Shiva mantra.

After a time that seemed like eternity, Bali finally landed on Rishyamukh Mountain. He dusted off the grime covering his body, preparing to dive into the Pampa. A deep voice from behind made him turn. He was astounded to see a handsome young man kneeling behind him, his face sullied and eyes red.

Well, this is what the folk artists sing. Bali was infamous for his pranks, keeping a straight face all the while and never missing a target.

'I accept defeat. You are the victor. Please grant a vanquished warrior the grace of death.' Ravan took out a dagger clasped to his waist belt and held it out to surrender.

Bali took some time to understand the message. 'In order for you to be defeated, shouldn't there at least be a war? I am the unfortunate one who can't claim the joy of defeating you as much as I would have loved to. I will not lie at this hour since I am in the middle of my prayers. If it were any other time of the day, I wouldn't mind.' He smirked.

There was something endearing about his voice. Ravan laughed out loud. We heard its echo across the forest. Rishyamukh quivered.

Sugreev approached the great bear Jambavan and a few others to accompany him in that direction. I stopped them. Somehow I had a feeling that everything was fine, no one needed to worry and no one should interfere. Sugreev needed to hear that. He quickly sat down, tense and praying for the safe return of his brother. I looked back in the direction of Rishyamukh Mountain, hoping to see some signs that confirmed my confidence. Even the crows had stopped cawing there.

'You may not have fought. But I was warring. And I have been brutally beaten. Quite literally. I deserve death. I can't go back and tell them that I survived a battle I lost. Please grant me the honour,' Ravan pleaded.

'Ho ... ho ... ho ... hold on,' Bali closed his arms. 'You want me to go back to my tribe and tell them that though I had nothing to do with someone, I killed him because he lost a hand in a battle which I didn't fight!' He stretched his back towards the right, then to the left. 'Ridiculous. It's below my dignity.' Without another word,

Bali dived into the Pampa Sarovar. The herons quacked and made way.

The water coughed with a reverse splash. Ravan had jumped in after him. They countered the currents with speed, propelling their arms back and forth, swooping inside the water and coming up again. Neither could swim faster than the other. In the middle of the lake, Ravan caught up with Bali and brought him to a halt.

'I am a warrior, Bali. I can't live with the shame of defeat,' he said, floating on the surface.

Bali leaned against a rock for a brief respite. 'Animals attack only when they are threatened. I am not scared of you, nor do I see you as an enemy who can cause harm to me or my clan.' Ravan sighed as Bali watched him, amused. 'This doesn't undermine your capability to do so; it only boasts of my power to protect my dependants. Why fight and kill when we can be friends?'

'A friendship between us?' Ravan was shocked. 'Do you know that I consider Indra, your father, to be my arch-rival?'

'Defeat and dismiss him if you can. I promise never to come in between.' Bali shrugged, standing in the water controlled by Indra.

The water level receded immediately. Neither of them cared. Ravan hugged Bali.

'I owe my life to you, my friend. You can claim it whenever you want,' he promised.

Why am I writing to you, Mandodari, about all this? The reasons are many. I'd never spoken to Ravan; he didn't know I existed. But these memories of him were left with me. Some I witnessed from a distance. The rest have passed on through the music and stories of the land. Consider this letter a handover of such memories.

We, the animals, operate with a freedom of our own. A friend we respect forever, an enemy we forget never. This ideology leaves me with certain obligations. For my family, Ravan was both a friend and an enemy – the former as pleasant as the latter was fierce. Though the friendship was mutual, our enmity towards Ravan was not direct. My clan and I got involved in a war which was not for the monkeys to fight and lose lives over.

However, for all living beings on this planet, ethics is a personal choice. Bali was a friend to Ravan; Sugreev became a friend of Ram. I served as the unspoken bridge between the twins, for this too, as in all other things.

Ravan must have told you about his friendship with Bali and the promise he made. Else, why would you respond to Bali's son, Angad, and thwart Ravan's life-saving yagna at a critical juncture of the war? Ravan may have forgotten his promise, you did not.

As for me, Mandodari, I believe Ram's strategic association with Sugreev wouldn't have helped him win the battle with Ravan, had he not been subtly aided by Bali's karma.

I end this letter with gratitude.

Yours,
Tara

1

I had seldom witnessed a more ferocious phase in my life. Heat waves had gripped the world. They melted the glaciers, unsettling Mahadev in Kailash. Blocks of ice surged into the Gangotri, flooding the plains below. Incendiary debris fell onto the turbulent surface, emitting thick smoke. Sea animals fled towards the sweet waters. Those who couldn't escape perished in the boiling waterbody that was once their trusted habitat. Fiery winds carrying a repulsive stench charged northwards, accusing the great god of severe injustice.

A forest fire had broken out on the outskirts of Kishkindha, and it was spreading fast. Our land, along with its residents, would be wiped out if the calamity was not contained right away. The *vanar* women rushed forward to throw water at the flames. The fire seemed to have opened its mouth with demonic hunger. The roasted flesh was insufficient for its insatiable gluttony. Only the rains could quench this inebriate.

'Rocks. Dump rocks!' I commanded. 'Keep up with the water.' I grabbed Bali's mace and rushed towards the Pampa. The girls stopped abruptly. Without wasting time, they divided themselves into three groups. One ran behind Ruma, balancing as many rocks on their heads and shoulders as they could. This task wasn't difficult; the forest, spread out on the plains beneath a mountain, was littered with stones of all shapes and sizes. The two other groups followed me.

We gathered water from the Pampa and hurled it at the fire with all our might. Another group collected a huge pile of leaves in no time. I closed my eyes and uttered a prayer: 'Forgive me, Mother Earth. We need to survive. We need resources. We have no other way.' With a heavy blow, I struck the dry earth using the mace. It shattered into powdery sand. The sand was scooped onto the large leaves and dropped on the flames from above, while water was splashed from the sides. In the meantime, the stones, both big and small, began to fall too.

The burning trees rustled out their last prayers. Some of the girls jumped atop them, scattering a cover of thorny leaves. Gel-like material was trapped between the blades of their large shoots. Oh god, I'd completely forgotten about them. This region grew these plants in plenty. The fire seemed to be receding. No one stopped until every last flicker was extinguished. Smoke swirled upwards, suppressed by the ambush. I looked at Ruma; she was already staring at me. We turned away before the tears could fall from our eyes.

*

'Let us uproot these useless plants,' Sugreev suggested.

'No,' Bali said sternly. 'We will not uproot anything. There must be an alternative.'

'But these are not edible,' argued Sugreev, tearing off a piece from the long, thorny leaves and shoving it into his mouth. Its slimy, watery membrane stuck to his tongue. 'Yuck!' He spat it out immediately. 'Atrocious. The edges hurt.'

'These plants will stay where they are. It's their space,' Bali affirmed. 'We will figure out another way to our food. I think Sushena can advise.'

Sushena, my father.

'He is a doctor, not an agricultural expert,' Sugreev grimaced.

Bali slapped his back, making his twin squirm. 'Mark my words, brother. Someday, in a moment of great crisis, these plants will provide crucial relief. Thank me then.'

Sugreev removed his brother's fingers from his aching back, grumbling to himself. 'Inedible plants will save us from an imaginary massacre. Doctors should double up as farmers. Animals must thrive in the wild, strictly partitioned from urban civilization. What's next? Fish will fly? Birds will burp? Butterflies will chew?' Sugreev grouched away. Bali headed leftwards to meet my father.

2

'What was this, Bali?' I asked. Tired and triumphant, the girls were going back now. The smoke from burnt leaves was suffocating. The smell was familiar – it had emerged from Bali's pyre not so long ago.

'Didn't I say these plants would save lives?' he bragged, missing the point as usual.

'When a prediction comes true, pride comes naturally. Self-obsession elevates it to another level.'

His laughter resounded through the scorched trees. 'The foolish receive the success of others with jealousy.'

I wished I could slap him. Instead, I went back to my question. 'Why this sudden heat and forest fire?'

'Oh, that,' he returned to the context. 'The war has

ended. Ram has achieved victory. Ravan is defeated. Sita is back.'

The information was delivered curtly, devoid of excitement. 'That is good news!' I exclaimed. 'Why is nature being so violent then?'

I heard a sigh, a deep one. 'As Ravan's pyre burns on the other side, there is a fire on this side too,' he paused. 'The fire of suspicion. Callous speculations have been launched at Sita like pointed arrows. They interlocked to raise a blazing rampart in her path. The arrows have flown in from all corners of the country, which has just been apprised of the great victory. They are sceptical about Sita's loyalty. What had she traded to stay alive in enemy land? They expect the fire to expose the woman's sins, if any.'

I cringed. 'Ram doesn't do anything? Lakshman doesn't protest? Sugreev? Hanuman?'

'They can't do anything,' Bali said calmly. 'Questions have answers. Attacks have a counter. Distrust is a black shadow cast by polluted minds. No one knows the origin; it is only felt in collective cynicism.'

I wanted to break some heads. What progress do the civilized gloat about if they cannot put their backyards in order? It's quite obvious why Bali had no respect for the principles of humans!

'What happened to Sita?' My voice was solemn, restraining my instinct from venting out at Bali.

He sounded warm now. 'She walked through the flames and came out unscathed. Silent as steel, answerable to none. The fire has lost its heat. But earthly environment is affected. Tranquil nature is angry.'

'Foolish world,' I remarked.

'Foolish or wise, such is it,' Bali interrupted. 'Beyond this dense forest lives a camp of chameleons. They change colours, their tongues venomous. They bite those who are kind. They withdraw and worship if their poison can't kill, waiting for an opportune time when their victims would be vulnerable.'

Bali often spoke in metaphors these days. He used to be more direct earlier. 'What does this mean?'

'Nothing,' he pulled back. 'Sita is fine. The humans call her Sita ma now, preparing to fall at her feet, seeking blessings from the goddess whom their fire could not burn.'

Goddess! I grabbed the branch of a tree between my fist, eventually loosening my grip.

'Where are you now, Bali?' I remembered his hands around my waist not too long ago.

Unaware of my thoughts, Bali killed the romance. 'At the edge of the sea, where the fire from the deceased king's pyre goes straight up to the sky.'

'Isn't Ravan with you by now?' I uttered, surprised.

'No. His pyre still burns. He hasn't left yet, not completely,' he observed. 'The celebrations have begun on the other side. Sita is no longer visible. The monkeys are rejoicing. Dussehra. The festival will henceforth commemorate the defeat of Ravan by Ram, the fall of the sinner before the godly.' In Bali's words, I could see what had transpired in Sugreev's troop. Their happiness was well-earned.

'You believe that Ravan was a sinner?' I tried to corner Bali, but he was a tough nut.

'Relationships don't make characters, actions do. Ravan kidnapped Sita and he killed Jataayu. No friendship should shield acts of crime.'

Well, I wasn't expecting this. I was yet to disown the bitterness, though. 'Shouldn't Dussehra also immortalize Sita's walk through the fire of suspicion?'

'For pessimists, it would. For optimists, not really.' He seemed to smile. 'Dussehra honours the love story of Sita and Ram, which remained steady despite domestic and foreign invasions.'

Bali left me curious. Arguments with the dead are seldom conclusive.

'They will be back in Kishkindha soon,' he added. 'Go, prepare.'

'Why should I believe in ambiguous information received from the lifeless?' I shrugged and started strolling back to the tribe. 'No one has told me anything; I haven't heard anything.'

Bali used to say that I am a difficult woman. It's fun being one.

3

Soon, the Pushpak chariot landed on the plains below Rishyamukh Mountain, sending the region's dwellers into a frenzy. Everyone ran to catch a glimpse of Ravan's famous birdcraft carrying the victors, the erstwhile hostage and Lanka's traitor, Vibhisan. I stood around lazily, watching the mayhem.

'Tara!' Ruma called out. 'What are you standing here for? Get ready, quick. We need to welcome them.'

Ruma, Sugreev's wife. I dragged her closer by the hand, arranging her hair and fur. 'You go. Sugreev will be with them.'

The girl was glowing with excitement. She

hesitated. 'Sugreev wouldn't appreciate it. You are the chief ...'

'Hierarchy be damned,' I snapped at her. 'Now run.' And she did. The attendants got busy arranging food and accommodations for the guests. Ruma had personally inspected the cave at Rishyamukh that Ram and Sita would occupy. Kishkindha was alive and buzzing after days of deafening quietness. I looked up at the sky. It felt as if Bali had returned after some expedition.

Soon after, I caught a whiff of him. He had taken another route to enter Kishkindha, tiptoeing forward as I leaned against a bamboo stem. Just as he lifted his hand mid-air, I raised mine and flipped the falling coconut shell back at him. He jumped back. 'How do you always know!'

I laughed and touched his chin. Angad, my son by Bali, swatted my hand away. He turned towards me, thumping the ground with his feet. I tickled him the way I used to when he was a child. He forgot everything, giggled and leapt forward to lift me with his right hand, tossing me upwards! I landed on his left shoulder. Carrying me in that position, he started jumping from one tree to another as I flicked his nose with my tail. By the time we parked, he was panting, as was I.

I wished this boy didn't remind me so much of Bali.

'Father never ran out of breath, I know,' he admitted, gasping and raising a hand to stop me.

I smiled. 'Your father would have thrown me to the grass. Sons are kinder than ...'

'Lovers?' He snatched my words midway, chuckling at the liberty he had just taken. When I picked up a bamboo shoot, he ran to save his head.

Angad went back to attend to the guests at Rishyamukh after our brief exchange. 'These diplomatic duties are a burden,' he pulled a face. 'Uncle Sugreev has become strict. He was easier when I was a child.'

'You still are,' I remarked, bidding him goodbye. Responsibilities influence priorities. He promised to be back soon.

Only once Angad had left did I realize that I was alone, breathing in a kingdom of ghosts.

The tall trees glanced down sadly. Everyone else had moved to Rishyamukh. The children and the elderly had soldiers to welcome home. Proud stories of war and victory would be shared. There were also soldiers to mourn, those who fought bravely for as long as they could. Sitting in my place, I could feel both the cheer and laments. Angad and Ruma must be there now, helping them balance the happiness and pain. Condolence hurts. Teasing visuals from the past and the tormenting stillness of the present stare blankly at a hopeless future.

*

Our vast forest was home to lazy owls that slept during the day and glared through the night. As soon as any of them managed to catch a frog, one rogue or another would alert the rest. Uninvited guests would flock to the feast. I had learnt their language when I was small. My shriek in broad daylight would cause some of them to remove the cover of their wings, only to realize that their hours were not over yet. Even the bears, vultures and monkeys turned when I called in owl-voice. The birds were certainly not pleased with the joke. As revenge, they tried to shit on me from above when I was busy daydreaming. Several summer hours were spent matching my misconduct with perverse rewards showered by the feisty owls.

Many afternoons ago, as Bali engaged in some profound discussion with the great bear, I hooted again. The owls flocked together, cursing and shitting from all directions. We called Jambavan 'the great bear'. The tall, broad, hairy animal sauntered back and forth, with his torso inclined forward, humming self-drafted songs if his tummy was full. He didn't want to be called Uncle or Grandfather, preferring to be addressed by his name – Jambavan. He growled at the fretting owls. Bali didn't bat an eyelid. Perhaps a soft smile appeared on the side of his lips. Nevertheless, there wasn't any response. Discouraged, I hooted more at the stupid birds and returned to the idle hours. Just as I sat still today. Not a leaf moved; life was silent. Leaning back, I closed my eyes, smiled and hooted. It had been long since I had last done it. The owls protested from their perches. The moments slipped away. Shadowed below the ketaki tree, I fell asleep.

A few hours must have passed. I woke up to the tremors of the soil. Not that I had anyone to fear. But who could be approaching at this hour? Not a four-pawed creature; this one was walking on two legs. I didn't move, pretending to be asleep. The walking stopped a yard away. There was no movement after that. The creature was very much there, though. I could smell it and hear it breathing. Not someone from this forest. In Kishkindha, everyone knew everyone. Even if we didn't, no one waited for formal introductions. We simply slid into each other's worlds. This creature was an epitome of patience. Could this be Sita? Cannot be anyone else!

I got up immediately.

In a dark corner right ahead of me, I saw the outline of someone sitting below a bamboo bush. My eyes widened. A woman, draped in *palash-*

coloured cotton cloth, rose quickly. I'd seen Ram and Lakshman in similar garments before. Leaves rustled behind her.

I slowly drew closer. She, too, walked forward. Between those steps taken towards each other, a lot flashed inside my mind. Ram had arrived because Sita was missing. Bali died because Ram had come. Why was Sita here now? What did she want?

Soon we were standing before each other. She was taller. Her fair skin looked rough and tanned. Beautiful eyes, not round like mine, were gentle. Neatly plaited hair, adorned with wild yellow *punnaga* flowers, hung loosely behind her. Ruma must have oiled her hair strands with the tree extracts. Those potions were available to all, though the source was tightly held by Ruma. She was the sole custodian of such remedial ingredients.

*

Every once in a while, Ruma would disappear without informing anyone, leaving old tongues wagging. Sugreev would be anxious and I, amused.

'Wife ran away, eh? Well, very sad. But why am I not surprised? She must have found someone more handsome.' I sat beside him with a straight face, patting his back in consolation for his shame and suffering.

Sugreev climbed up a coconut tree to look around; Ruma was nowhere to be found. He kept sitting there nervously, unwilling to come down to my buffoonery. Bali was passing by. He found me standing below with hands on my waist and his brother atop the tree. Stretching his body to the right and then to the left, he joined us.

'What happened? Come down, brother, don't worry. Ruma will never leave you,' he assured. Sugreev looked down immediately with expectant eyes. 'At best, she will flirt around for a while and return when she is satisfied. Only fools abandon a tamed mate for a feral fancy. Ruma is no fool.'

Sugreev broke some green coconuts and let them fall. We back-flipped before the fruits hit our heads, laughing hysterically.

Ruma returned late in the afternoon. The elderly monkeys, who had been gossiping until then, went quiet. Sugreev thumped the ground, seeking answers. The young girl gently placed a hand on his chest and shut him down for good.

'Where was she?' I didn't speak, but my eyes must have asked much more than a simple question. I was certain that Bali was aware. He shrugged, raising his shoulders up to his ears.

'Magic of the monkeys. Abundance of the forest. That's all I know. Whoever discovers it, owns it.' Bali looked affectionately at the couple walking away, hand in hand. A bunch of yellow punnaga flowers hung carelessly from her waist.

Those flowers were adorning Sita today.

They were the flowers that Ruma had brought to cover Bali's dead body.

Did she love the yellow punnaga, or hate them? Were they filled with good wishes, or did they carry her poison? It was a secret that Ruma would never disclose, and I would never ask.

4

After a long monsoon, the weather was lethargically proceeding towards autumn. Days were getting shorter. The creepers and the shrubs engaged in cryptic conversations all through the day about discarding the obsolete for new beginnings. They reminded the palash trees to bear buds a little before time and announce the advent of spring quicker. The animals yawned and moaned. Eyes half-closed, the great bear swayed as if he were listening to some chants. The squirrel nesting in the hole of the tree slipped and fell on his head. He wasn't bothered. The little thing rubbed its eyes, realized where it was and scurried back to its hole before Jambavan could lay his fingers on it. I wouldn't have laughed if Ruma hadn't first. Jambavan raised his head, looked at us with drooping eyes, acquitted us of an offence we weren't regretting, and went back to swaying his head to the imaginary rhythm.

'What have you done to him?' I asked Ruma. She laughed more.

'What to do?' she uttered between hiccups. 'Last night, he suddenly came to meet the doctor. Yes, your father, who else?' She lowered her voice. 'Started asking obnoxious questions, testing my knowledge in medicine. Kept enquiring about the cure for bone injuries in the arms and knees. The difference between the bone structure of arms and knees – he didn't know.'

Jambavan could be really irritating at times. He'd go around to examine the expertise of others and share hypothetical solutions for problems he knew nothing about. There was hardly a monkey or a bear in these lands who had not been stopped by him for a discussion on topics ranging from galaxies in the sky to the food available in the northern ice lands, the architecture of kingdoms oceans apart, to the underworld refineries governed by the Asur. But he was kind, lovable and grandfatherly. My favourite playmate until I learnt to crawl over and fight with peers over bananas. Even then, he would take my side and accuse others of cheating in the games.

'The more I answered and explained, the more inquisitive he became.' Ruma's words ran a scissor through my well-restored images from childhood. '*How would you treat a monkey suffering from both a sore throat and diarrhoea? The throat needs something warm and the belly calls for something cold. What would you do?*' Ruma mimicked the old bear. 'Now I had to stop him and get back to my stuff, eh?'

'So?' Though a wave of laughter was gurgling inside me, I asked seriously.

Ruma drew closer to whisper, 'I had stored some *datura* paste in the vacated squirrel hole of the blackest branch on the north-west of the third sal from here.'

'What!' I couldn't believe my ears. 'You gave datura to the great bear?'

She looked around and winked. 'Not raw. I mixed it with other herbs. A few days of peace for all.' Ruma started walking away.

I knew how to get her to walk backwards. 'Father knows?'

She whirled around. 'Come on, Tara.'

I shrugged. One complaint would throw her out of his company. Ruma was the cause of many a scolding I'd received from Father, primarily owing to my indifference towards medical science.

'Ruma is a genius,' he'd say whenever I was within earshot. 'Seldom have I seen such soulful dedication at such a young age. Her brain is born for discoveries, her hands blessed to heal. Wish others showed half the enthusiasm.'

His *other* would be caught up in decoding the sounds of the night. Or learning the language of sparrows. Father Sushena would cast a disgusted look at the choices I made with my time. 'What a sheer waste!' he'd lament.

Here was Father's 'genius', serving datura to his best friend because he asked too many questions. Why should I let go of the opportunity?

'Tara, listen.' Ruma somersaulted towards me. 'I have the recipe of a divine syrup. Sweeter than honey. I can give that to you. The entire tub,' she tried to buy my silence. When I didn't show any interest, she gave up. 'Fine, tell me what you want.'

'Your secrets,' I pronounced my price.

'Tara!' she exclaimed. 'What will you do with medical information?'

Practically, nothing. I only wanted access. When I didn't answer, she started bargaining. 'One, only.'

'No way, at least five,' I argued. Nothing could persuade her to raise the number. Between nothing and one, I chose the latter.

'*Ashwagandha* mixed with eucalyptus extract and tulsi leaves can reduce exhaustion and reenergize miraculously. Vanjula flowers added to the mixture will cleanse the stomach. I heard the sages dwelling at Rishyamukh discussing vanjula,' she disclosed one of her discoveries that had been approved by Father. 'Ashwagandha plants grow sporadically in the far west of the forest. Eucalyptus and tulsi are in abundance. Only vanjula is missing.'

When she started discussing proportions and recipes, I lost interest. But Ruma held me by the hand. 'Tara, would you help me find vanjula plants?'

Eh, so much for my father's brilliant disciple. She chose a secret to seek a favour. I felt like such a loser. Ruma really knew how to price up a free offer. I gritted my teeth and mentioned that I would think about it, before returning to my abode, where an unhappy father was waiting for his worthless daughter. 'Mend your ways. Everyone says the doctor raised a mad girl ...' were the last words I heard from him before falling asleep.

*

'Father, do you feel it?' I asked, sitting up. It was still dark outside.

A few jumps away, Father had woken up too. 'Earthquake?'

'Not an earthquake. Something else. Like

marching footsteps,' I said anxiously. Father was worried, as was I.

Soon, more monkeys and bears joined us, afraid and concerned. Although we had never been attacked before, we acutely knew the perils of a sudden strike. We were a bunch of unarmed animals with only claws and sharp teeth at our disposal. Hanuman was our only guardian, but he was often away meditating or serving those in need. Of course, we had bamboo poles and tree branches if necessary. Ruma possessed a limited supply of lethal concoctions. These weren't enough.

I looked around for any semblance of preparations. From the edge of the Pampa Sarovar, they emerged. Not a regiment of soldiers, rather two large monkeys. One was carrying the other on his shoulder. The rider was fast asleep as the bearer took broad steps forward, anxious and gasping from exhaustion. Sleep-deprived eyes had sunken into an ashen face. Looked like he had been travelling since ages.

Brother Hanuman joined us with his father, Kesari, and mother, Anjani. I stepped back to stand behind them, along with many others, paying respect to the elders. With Hanuman leading, we paraded forward. The huge monkey didn't notice us. He dove into the Pampa, drinking water as if enduring a drought within himself. He got up eventually, water filled in his palms, and started pouring it into the mouth of the other monkey, who was lying motionless on the track. His hands shook, and so did we. Spectacularly alike, these were twins.

'Stop!' A sharp response came from our side, startling the huge monkey. 'You will choke him. Move aside.'

Ruma ran towards them, ignoring everyone else. My father followed her. We waited with bated breath. 'Breathing, not dead,' my father announced after checking. Ruma disappeared for a bit and came back with green, juicy coconuts. She lifted the monkey's numb head carefully and started feeding him coconut water. After a long, deafening silence, he opened his eyes and started sneezing. Countless times. His twin sprang up, his worry replaced with anger, kicking his brother on the back.

'I am the one carrying his weight for a full monsoon and more, and he faints. I bathe in freezing water, and this one starts to sneeze. Tell me one quality which makes you my brother.'

Before Father could intervene, the seated one rejoindered in a subdued voice, 'I am chasing a mirage with a lunatic day after day. And then—'

'Mouth shut!' the other one yelled. By now, he had noticed the rest of us. He approached Ruma, holding her hands between his. God knows whether it was to express gratitude or an attempt to speak. My father cleared his throat from behind and Ruma stepped back, releasing her hand. The monkey turned towards us. His brother stood up too, dusting off the grass on his back.

'So many monkeys. And a few bears. That's it?' the elder one wondered aloud. Hazel eyes blinked rapidly, warm and enthusiastic, unlike the drooping ones of his twin.

'Lots of birds too, in case you'd consider borrowing their wings for the rest of your journey. Walking troubles the weak-hearted,' I blurted out in a shaky voice, pretending to faint. A chorus of laughter erupted from the gathering. Some of them mouthed merry sounds, teasing the new targets.

The eastern sky was clearing up. Two pairs of eyes fell upon me along with the first rays of the sun. The elder one looked naughty, vibrant and intense. Behind him, the duplicate was cold and stern, somewhat melancholic, questioning my right to ridicule.

'Someone, please give them something to eat. Else, the other one will collapse, and there is no spare shoulder to carry him,' I said to no one in particular.

One pair of eyes was amused. His twin jumped thrice, muttering about etiquette and audacity. 'We don't want anything,' he declared, thumping his feet on the ground.

'Of course you don't,' I crushed his vanity like an earthworm under my thumb. 'Two coconuts have already made their way down your throat. You aren't starving!'

Sunlight had spread everywhere by now. The elder one called for peace. 'Some food would be really good. She is right. I am starving.'

Hanuman and his father intervened quickly, apologizing for not having offered adequate hospitality to the walk-ins. For a while, I stood enjoying the spectacle. From the corner of his eye, the elder one kept glancing my way. I slipped away before someone could depute me with the unwanted tasks of attending to the guests.

'Don't feel bad about what she said, son,' I heard my father say while befriending the strangers. 'Every tribe has its own malicious *pishachini*. She is ours.'

On the other side of the forest, I had halted the *chakravak* birds. These were lover birds, unwilling to call any place their permanent home. Whether they loved their partner or life itself was debatable. Lost unto each other, they composed unwavering ballads praising beaks and feathers, their moments of togetherness and the memories they were creating. I listened carefully – learning and noting. By evening, I had mastered their language. Their voice, the pitch and their songs. Impressed by my devotion, the chakravaks blessed that I would have an exciting love life, that even death would not separate me from my lover. Which woman would not be thrilled? I sat idly, dreaming of a faceless lover, coyed by the pishachini among the monkeys.

Ruma came panting when the sun had started its descent. She lay flat on the ground beside me. 'You are always the cunning one, Tara,' she complained.

'I am sure it is a compliment. So, why this generosity?' I remarked, my eyes fixed on the crimson sky.

'By feeding coconut water to a grown-up child, I have rewarded myself with the role of their caretaker. "Ruma, this … Ruma that". Their needs are dumped on me like falling mangoes in the monsoon storm while others lounge around listening to their travel tales,' she ranted. 'Stop laughing!'

I looked at my tired friend and caressed her forehead softly. 'If a forest has a pishachini, let it have its apparitions too.' We both chuckled.

'Giant-bodied, and looking alike; the only difference is that one is timid, dominated by a fascinating elder,' Ruma echoed.

The sun had dipped below the horizon. The trees were dozing off, their heavy breaths whispered eerie prophecies of forgotten curses resurfacing. 'Let's go.' Ruma pulled me up. 'You know what?' she uttered unmindfully as we walked back. 'I have a hunch that Sugreev didn't faint. He just wanted to be carried and faked the rest.'

This was interesting. 'Really! That's smart,' I slowed my pace to concentrate better. 'What is the name of the elder one?'

Ruma brought me up to speed again. 'Sugreev is not smart. Just afraid. He must have requested Bali to stop and rest. I suspect his brother had been unwilling for reasons best known to him. Unable to protest, Sugreev put up an act.'

When we reached our dwelling, the two guests were enjoying bananas, looking refreshed after a good sleep. The others circled around them. Moonlight sieved intermittently through the canopy of the sleeping trees above.

'Tara!' Hanuman was the first to notice and greet me.

One of the twins turned at his voice. Innocent face, playful smiles, hazel eyes. 'Tara,' he repeated after Hanuman, 'an unexpected name for a pishachini.'

This had to be Bali. I smiled back sweetly, silently pledging to show him every star of the night sky in broad daylight.

*

'Tara?' The woman in front brought me back from the random images of the past.

'Sita!' I paused, wondering what to say and how. 'What brings you here?' I wished I didn't have to see her.

Sita may have read that her unsolicited advent had not been heartily welcomed. She took two steps back.

'I came to meet the queen of Kishkindha,' she said sceptically. 'I've heard a lot about you. So ...'

'Heard about me! From whom?' I couldn't help asking. Her answer was not something I was in the least prepared for.

'Lakshman, my brother-in-law.' She allowed me some moments to process this information. What on earth did Lakshman know about me? Before I could ask, Sita spoke again. 'He'd often say that Kishkindha runs on the brains of Sugreev's wife—'

'I am Bali's widow, unless Sugreev needs me for political exigencies,' I cut her short. Were all humans cruel or was it only their men?

'Yes, true. I stand corrected,' she quickly conceded. Awkward stillness pervaded between us. I decided to honour the guest.

'Still not scared of venturing into the forest alone?' I changed my tone, referring to the recent calamity she had endured.

She smiled, meeting my gaze. 'The forest has always been kind to me. Birds and animals, plants and hermits – everyone has helped in every way they could. Danger came from outside the forest, yet the benign has caught infamy.'

Touched, I looked at the woman from head to toe. Simple and calm, she carried a distancing radiance. How could Ravan not foresee that this radiance would one day smoulder him to death?

5

Father may have been right. I was indeed the pishachini among monkeys. Why else would I eavesdrop on conversations not meant for me? It wasn't that I always wanted to do so. Secrets volunteered to be peeled away if I didn't chase them.

Late at night when the forest was silent, the elders gathered for a discreet meeting: Father Sushena, Jambavan, Anjani ma and Uncle Kesari. Though seated afar, their whispers found me when I was busy relieving my itching ears with a supple green stem.

'The boys are intelligent,' my father said. 'The elder one, especially.'

'Of what use would they be to us, Sushena?' Jambavan asked.

'We need our successors.' Father was excited. 'These two can add to the might of the monkeys.'

'Why them? What's wrong with our native monkeys?' Uncle Kesari was surprised.

'They are strong-bodied,' Father reasoned. 'The elder one is a fast thinker, with unwavering faith in the primordial wisdom of animals. I like that.'

Anjani ma agreed. 'The younger one is also good, but he is clueless without his brother. Bali is sharp. I think they are on a mission. They are looking for something.' Everyone stared at her inquisitively. 'No, neither of them told me. It is just an intuition. I could be wrong.'

Everyone went silent. Anjani ma was never wrong. Her words were absolute, even if spoken unintentionally. The gossip in the forest went that passing winds left the bulletins at her doorstep.

'Is this true, Anjani ma? Is there something sizzling between you and the wind god?' I had once poked her.

'Muck on your tongue, boorish woman,' she had cursed angrily. 'Smear ginger on your own face.'

The scandal certainly had its root somewhere, I deduced; else she wouldn't have bothered. When she saw me chuckling, she cursed some more.

'So why are we meeting?' Uncle Kesari broke the silence.

'Sushena wants us to retain them here,' Jambavan spoke after a long time. 'For the safety of the tribe.'

'Which means,' Uncle Kesari said slowly, 'we will have to stop them from pursuing their mission, whatever it may be?' He looked at the others; 'yes' was written on each of their faces.

Father inched closer to him. 'Brother Kesari, the forest is our beloved homeland. But danger lurks at every step. Days are changing; ferocious *rakshas* and menacing *daitva* roam capriciously. Just a few days ago, young Nal and Nil were playing on the outskirts when they spotted the horrifying Dunduvi loitering around, eyeing the forest. This is not good news.'

Dunduvi. Son of Maya, the Asur architect; brother to Mayavi and Mandodari, the queen of Lanka. I frowned; I had seen him too, peeping from the other side of the dense forest, searching for God knows what. The migratory birds from the west reported that the delinquent youth fancied lifting girls by force. Hadn't the mighty Ravan impressed his headstrong sister by abducting her?

'Quite risky,' Uncle Kesari nodded.

Father had bigger concerns. 'You know Tara, Brother. Goes wandering without telling anyone, lazing around wherever she pleases. A disaster of a woman – laughs at anything, rubs just about anyone the wrong way. If the monster were to come after her—'

'Tara!' Anjani ma interjected. 'Even a monster would have better taste, Sushena. I'd worry about Ruma if I have to. Not Tara,' she laughed.

My father wasn't pleased. He couldn't be offended at Anjani ma's dismissal either. I was indeed their problem child.

'Ruma knows how to use the forest reserves

to her advantage. Tara refuses to learn,' Father complained. 'I had given Tara some datura poison to numb predators. She buried it for safekeeping under a mango tree – which one, she has forgotten! Once I caught hold of her as she was heading out and placed another pack in her palm. She lost it somewhere on the way. You tell me what I should do with her,' Father lamented.

I smiled, keeping my eyes tightly shut.

Anjani ma was about to respond when Jambavan stopped her. 'So, where were we? What do we say to stop these two, and how can they help?'

'Maybe they can stay with us and guard the forest from foreign vices,' Father suggested.

'Hehehe,' Jambavan started laughing suddenly, taking his audience by shock. 'The doctor wants the boys to live in this forest as our slaves because they are strong and one seems more intelligent than all of us! I am sure they would be delighted.'

I was laughing my heart out too, with hands over my mouth to stifle any sound.

'I can't provide all the solutions,' Father said, irritated. '*What*, I told you. *How*, you decide.'

Jambavan continued laughing. Anjani ma came up with an idea.

'Sushena is right.' All ears turned towards her. The great bear hiccupped twice and then stopped for good. 'Not slavery;, we will offer leadership. Ask Bali to rule over the terrain and become the king of this forest. It would be a good incentive for them to consider.'

Uncle Kesari agreed. 'We are the older generation. It is time for the youth to take over. The reclusive Hanuman would never agree to take charge. Bali is a good choice.'

In just a day, the elders had decided to hand over the reins of their land to strangers. Didn't I say that we, the animals, act on impulse?

While one corner of the forest was abuzz with detention plans, another conspired of freedom. The giants were awake. Curious, I switched sides to gather what was happening there.

Bali threw his leg on a happily sleeping Sugreev.

'Eeeeeeehhh! You hurt my belly. Remove

your weight, elephant!' Sugreev grunted drowsily, trying to push his brother's leg away with both hands.

'Grow up and get up, softy.' Bali smirked as he withdrew.

'Don't call me that,' Sugreev protested, 'and let me sleep.'

'You seem to have settled well here.' Bali kicked his twin's raised knee. Sugreev's long limb flopped onto the grass. 'We must leave soon. This is not our home.'

'There is no such thing called home, Brother. You have to make one.' Sugreev turned and buried his face in the leaves on the ground. 'Accept it, Bali,' he uttered again when he didn't hear anything back. 'She is gone for good. You and I have searched enough. We should have found her by now. We haven't because she doesn't want to be found.'

My ears perked up. Was there a love story? Who could it be? A wife? A lover? Bali's lover?

'Ruma reminds me of her. The same healing touch. The eternal caregiver.' Bali didn't hear his brother.

'This is getting murkier,' I thought. Sugreev taunted – the exact same words, at the same time. His sleep had disappeared. Only Sugreev earned another kick for it. I chuckled from a safe distance.

'I won't give up.' There was an edge of madness to Bali's voice that could be detected even by the deaf. 'He has imprisoned her. The coward. Cruel. It showed on his face. She must be in pain. I need to go.' Bali sat up.

'It is her life, Bali. Who are we?' Sugreev sat up behind him. 'We cannot interfere unless we are called.'

'Stop thinking like a human,' Bali dismissed. 'I suspect he hasn't left her in a position to call out. Else I would have heard her, if not you.' Bali's voice was drenched in agony. 'I will interfere. The rules of humans are not applicable to us.' He thumped his feet.

Who was this mysterious woman? Who was her culprit? How could two able-bodied males not help her? Questions were many, answers none. I nearly stood up to join them, demanding

I be told everything in detail. There must be something I could do!

'Calm down, Bali.' Sugreev was softly patting his brother's shoulder now, like one does to reason with little children. 'I am always with you. I will go as far as you want me to.' He hugged Bali. 'All I am saying is, let's not keep travelling without a plan. We have been searching for ages. We need some time to stop and think. This is the best place for it. Please consider.'

Lying on the grass with a hand covering my face, I glanced at the brothers. Bali waited for a while, looking upwards, his eyes locked into a void. 'I know why you want to stick around here. Don't even think about it.' He sounded serious. 'You will be mashed into a pulp or crunched up like seeds.'

'What! Who? Why?' Sugreev sat apart and looked at Bali's face, passive and tensed. I, too, was curious to hear about the new villain in this story.

'The notorious Tara.' An irritating smile touched Bali's eyes.

'Why would she crush me?' Sugreev was defensive now. I also stiffened.

'You end up falling in love with the ones who annoy you.' Bali laughed.

'Ginger juice-fed maggot, you rotten-tailed ...!' Sugreev immersed himself in the pleasure of abusing his twin. I put out my hand. A bamboo stick lying near my head whirled diagonally upwards and banged against a bunch of juicy coconuts waiting to grow the fruit inside their belly. Bali sprang up and pushed Sugreev out of the way. With a thud, the cluster fell between them. Shaken, Sugreev caressed his head and thanked the gods for sparing it in one piece.

'Seems the pishachini of the forest is awake.' Bali stretched himself. 'I am going for my prayers.'

'Wait, I am coming along with you. I won't stay here alone.' Sugreev followed him.

'Softy,' Bali ridiculed again.

'I am not,' Sugreev protested. 'It is intelligent to avoid insanity.'

The forest was waking up. The trees yawned, sending a cool morning breeze. It was going to be an interesting day. The guests would want to leave, but the elders would try to convince them otherwise. I had planned to work on my script – discovering the origin of sounds and appropriate symbols to represent them. Symbols existed amidst nature: the curve of trees, the beauty of flowers, the proboscis of butterflies, the beaks of birds and the flow of water. I selected the illustrations worth featuring and discarded the ones that looked difficult. A pictorial depiction was an option but that wouldn't be a script. I wanted our own script – a distinct calligraphy encrypted with the identities of the wild. I decided to put this work on hold for the time being. The comedy unfolding in this part of the forest was not worth missing. Ruma looked at me suspiciously. She'd rarely seen me so quiet, seemingly unhurried to disappear into my own world. I winked at her.

'How are my patients today?' she enquired with a smile when the two giants were back.

'You can swing ripe fruits from dead plants,'

Bali flirted. Ruma blushed. Sugreev frowned, and so did I. *Well!*

The elders appeared soon, with delicious bananas, dates, nuts, apples, berries, honey and everything else they could get. I pressed my lips together to stop myself from bursting into laughter. Sugreev was delighted. Bali looked at me quizzically, assuming something was cooking. Our surroundings were abuzz with everyone attending to the guests. Sugreev burped.

'Ruma, take them out. Give them a tour of the forest,' Uncle Kesari offered.

'Of course, why not? I was born to serve strangers,' Ruma mumbled softly. I chuckled. She tried to slap me. I moved away, leaving her palm to take a swift turn in the air. 'Why don't they ever ask you?' she asked, getting up and hitting the ground with her feet.

'Sugreev, you go with Ruma,' Bali said suddenly. 'I will sleep a little.'

Sugreev got up. Ruma looked disappointed.

'Of course, please rest,' Anjani ma smiled. 'We will see you later. Ruma can show Sugreev around.' The elders cleared the ground, so that the smart monkey could sleep peacefully. I grimaced. This was quite uneventful, compared to my expectations. Bali lay down and covered his eyes with his hand.

Sugreev and Ruma were walking away. She was unusually calm. Sugreev was trying to strike up a conversation. As I prepared to leap forward, I felt something. My head turned to find a pair of hazel eyes blinking at me from below the cover of muscular arms, as if gesturing for me to stay put. A coy smile crossed my lips. The prey had come on his own; the pishachini was ready to feast. The elders of the tribe were walking towards the mango forest, talking softly among themselves. I stopped. As soon as they were no longer visible, Bali sat up. 'What was this? The awkward over-attention?'

'A future planning device,' I announced. 'Why do you ask me?'

'Because you are the only one who knows. Ruma doesn't. I can see it on your face.' Bali leaned against the tree behind him.

'Let me rephrase my question.' I said, leaning against the tree behind me, imitating him. 'Why should I tell you?'

*

Right across the Pampa Sarovar, where the forest was denser and the ground was moist, the birds and the insects were raising a ruckus. Sugreev stopped abruptly. 'What happened to them?'

Ruma nodded. 'They are Tara's friends, thundering because she isn't here yet.'

'But why?' Sugreev bent slightly to hear from Ruma.

'She teaches them her language and learns theirs in return.'

'Incredible,' he replied, impressed. 'Just that she is too rowdy. Unnecessarily rebellious. Unpredictable.'

'Is your brother not?' Ruma threw the words right in his face and walked ahead as her tourist trailed behind.

6

For a long time that night, Bali didn't sleep. Beside him, his twin was wide awake. Despite being far from them, I too was sleepless. Some nights are futile. You must let them be. Drops of dew cascaded from the leaves, strumming a monotonous lullaby. The owls screeched from above, tempting me to grasp at an incomplete argument. The lump in my throat was hurting. I hated myself for it. 'It doesn't matter. Whether the twins live or die, shout or remain mute – nothing changes,' I told myself a thousand times. Yet the distress wouldn't subside.

Bali was furious this morning when I asked about his lover. When nice souls get angry, they appear all the more intimidating. 'None of your business,' he said slowly. 'Stay out of it. Who do you think you are?'

Resistance was expected, but the harshness was abrupt. No one had ever treated me like that. Unable to comprehend how to deal with the situation, and somewhat frightened, I leapt away. He did not call me back. I returned at night when everyone was busy with their chores. Bali still refused to look at me. Not that I was interested in his gaze either. But I was upset, and he did not care to apologize.

'Do you believe it?' Sugreev whispered to his twin. 'They call her a pishachini! She is a master of languages, trying to develop a script for the monkeys. Unbelievable.'

Bali didn't say anything. 'All life forms manage to communicate with each other in some way or the other. But Tara? She talks to a bird like a bird. She talks to a reptile like a reptile. She talks to an insect ...' Sugreev kept on blabbering praises before his aloof brother.

'I can't believe he agreed so easily,' came the

voices of the elders from the other side. I covered my ears with my hands. I didn't want to hear any further. Strange were the rules of the maker who had designed the animal anatomy to be so vigilant to external stimuli.

'He didn't agree,' Anjani ma corrected my father. 'He just bought time. "I will think about it" is far from a yes.'

If only I could have absolute silence when I wanted it most. I sprang up, climbed the trees, startled some sleeping birds, jumped from branch to branch and fled afar, searching for serenity. Where I was headed, I did not know.

The trees crowding the woodlands dropped their seeds for more of their kind to grow. We animals sometimes carried the fruits and dispersed the seeds. So the forest's composition did not adhere to systematic sectoring. However, various stretches had their own dominant growths, with the seeds falling and germinating. Certain distinct regions were labelled indicating their prevailing vegetations, for convenient referring. Traversing through them, I halted where the datura flowers were scattered under large sal trees. This part of the forest was abandoned and, hence, quieter. The intoxicating smell of the datura left my head spinning. A long sleep was my only respite from reality. Drowsy eyes came together. I wrapped my hands and legs around a sal. The tree groaned, as did the datura leaves on the ground, prompting me to move from there. I ignored their warnings. Resting my head against the trunk of the sal, eyes overflowing with tears and lower lip sticking out, I broke down. How dare he point a finger at me? Who was he to tell me to go away? This was my forest!

When I opened my eyes, my father was sitting nervously near my head. He was about to scold but Ruma stopped him. Wiping the sweat from his forehead, he walked away.

'Why were you there, Tara?' she asked calmly.

'My wish,' I snapped at her.

'Did you chew some straw or a seed?' she asked again. I had. A few of the pods had been long enough to brush against my mouth. I started nibbling on them before I passed out. I kept that to myself.

'Are you mad, Tara?' she said, taking my silence as agreement. 'For two days, you were gone. We looked for you everywhere, until Bali found you reclined over a sal, unconscious.'

I closed my fingers into a fist. Ruma's eyes bore into mine. 'He carried you back in his arms, a datura weed still dangling from your lips.'

I thumped the floor as many times as I could. My limbs felt feeble. The next instant, I was rubbing my palms around my arms and waist to erase any remnants of the touch. 'He carried me! And everyone just watched?' I was aghast. 'Not a single monkey commanded him to back off?'

'One slap to your face!' Ruma exclaimed angrily. 'Ungrateful woman.'

Ruma wouldn't understand, and I couldn't explain it to her. We sat in silence. Anjani ma entered, carrying fruits. 'Pishachini,' she muttered, disgusted. 'Feed her this so we won't be graced with the good fortune of lighting her pyre by the Pampa,' she said to Ruma before leaving as hastily as she'd entered. Ruma peeled a banana for me. A noise from behind made us both turn. I looked away immediately, preparing to spring forward and disappear again for good.

'I am Sugreev, Tara. Not Bali,' a soft voice floated in.

Oh, its Sugreev. Not Bali. Then play the drums and let's dance! How was it different when one twin looked just like the other? 'Get lost,' I said roughly.

Looks were exchanged between Sugreev and Ruma. She went to perform her chores, leaving me with the younger monkey. I wish she knew a little more about comforting than just administering medicines.

'Tara,' Sugreev pleaded, sitting a few steps away. 'I want to learn the language of the forest. Will you teach me? Please don't say no.'

I was stumped. This was news. So, he wasn't here with some friendly message from Bali? Whatever it was, he had earned my attention. 'Why?'

'I want to work with you on the script you are developing. Consider it. Two heads are better than one.' He smiled. This time, I adjusted my posture to observe him properly. He looked sincere.

'Wouldn't you have to leave soon?' I asked, without mentioning his brother. But Sugreev was not a fool.

'You shouldn't have broached it with him, Tara,' his voice flowed like warm sunlight on a chilly winter day. The anger, the insult, the sadness – and something more ineffable – it all started to come back. My ears were burning, my hands shaking.

'He wanted to know a secret. I asked for one in return – a simple transaction. What's wrong with that?' I blurted out.

Sugreev continued gently, 'Some secrets are not funny. They can't be shared simply by passing on the information. They are tied to one's existence. Painfully and emotionally. Bali is the emotional one, I am more reserved.'

'Don't defend your brother.' I felt a deep urge to strike him with my tail.

'Oh, I thought I was praising myself. Let it go.' He shrugged. 'May I please advise you to never bring this up again? It is a request, an important one.'

God knows what the twins were hiding as if it were the nectar of life. Rage spilled from my eyes as tears. 'Everyone in the forest thinks I'm a spoilt brat, born to bury the fame of her father in deep sand,' I sniffled. 'But I'm also their pampered child. They scold me, they also love me. Remind your arrogant brother that this land has extended kind hospitality to two outsiders.' I quickly wiped away my tears so that Sugreev wouldn't misunderstand. 'Who cares about his temper? Tell him to drown himself. I will hand out ripe bananas at his funeral.'

This man was patient. Empathetic too. Didn't try to explain his brother's actions, didn't reveal he had seen me crying. War can be between two disagreeing souls. When one of them doesn't have an opinion and is unwilling to judge, the arms feel undervalued. I calmed down. 'Who else knows about this?'

'No one,' he said. 'Who would Bali confide in?'

'He told you,' I pointed out.

'He didn't,' Sugreev corrected, to my surprise. 'Nothing else can disturb him as much. I guessed what must have happened. Whatever I just gathered is from you.'

*

Father's treatments and Ruma's care got me back on my feet soon. My head felt lighter. I swapped sleeping spots with Ruma.

'Did you sleep well last night?' I asked in the morning.

'Oh yes, it is better at your end. The insects by my old bed had made life hell.' She stroked her fingertips across my palm. I smiled.

'Do you think I could have died?' I wouldn't have believed her if the answer was yes.

'Worse,' she replied. 'An overdose of datura can cause blurred vision, hallucinations, anxiety or fever, leading to brain haemorrhage. All of which means that you wouldn't be dead, but you wouldn't be alive either.'

'Can't medical science respond in monosyllables?' Her thorough explanation had unnerved me.

'Medical science is not language that you can spread or restrict at will,' she teased.

When Ruma went off to work, I started walking around. The trees in the forest were happy to see me back, dropping a fruit or a flower as I crossed. Winter was setting in. My skin was getting drier. And my fur stood up when the morning breeze raced past. The marks I had left on the ground documenting my script had been destroyed by the hours of my absence. But I remembered them. Using a pointed stick, I drew the patterns again and lay back on the dry leaves, looking up at the sky and thinking.

Someone cleared his throat nearby. I jumped up.

'May I join you?' Sugreev asked with a smile. He observed the patterns I had made on the ground and asked a few questions about them for clarity.

'Humans are clever,' he remarked. 'They have identified some basic sounds and some complicated ones. They have recorded their extensions too. Semi-geometrical patterns are used to represent them, so that learning and remembering is not only easy but also logical,' he explained, looking at my designs. 'Your script is creative. I see many sketches here and there. Of objects. It would be restrictive unless you find a way to express emotions. For example, how do you write "love"?' he asked, seeming nervous about his unplanned boldness. The face could compete with a bursting plum. 'Or ... err, say for example ... let me think.' He was struggling to continue. I pinched myself to suppress the bubbling laughter. 'Anger, yes, anger. How do you show anger? A slap or a frown is not necessarily anger. Do you get my point?'

'You are right,' I pondered over it, trying to strike a solution. 'Let the objects be horizontal in our script then, the emotions vertical? The action signs could be diagonal?' I said with excitement.

'Great idea. Let's see how it works,' Sugreev

encouraged. We crafted our sentences, agreeing and disagreeing on the patterns, while making a genuine effort to keep them simple. After hours of indulgence, he stopped me. 'Tara, you need to rest.'

I truly did. We took a break from the tough task at hand. He requested me to communicate something in bird language – any bird – and explain the meaning. It was noon. I mimicked the owls. The sleeping monsters cursed us from above. No interpretation was needed. We both laughed our hearts out.

Time passed. Sugreev became a constant presence, sometimes like a disciple, other times as a teacher. Then there were days when he didn't speak at all. Mum throughout, whatever be asked – distanced and deep in thought. Animals have their moods; there was nothing bizarre about it. He stopped me from scripting words on the ground, instead plucking large leaves. I was taught to pierce the leaves carefully with pointed wooden sticks so they wouldn't tear while we were imprinting the words. Every evening, we walked back together. Whenever Bali was around, I turned away, unwilling to see his face or show him mine. I couldn't avoid his voice, though.

'Time is running out in inaction,' he'd lament to his brother. Each time when he prepared to leave our land, the elders distracted him with a new problem. Dunduvi had started visiting again. When he heard, Bali rushed towards him with a war cry and chased him beyond Rishyamukh. As winter set in, some animals were preparing to hibernate. Bali surveyed the forest within half a day and reported unexplored fruits and vegetables growing in remote stretches of the land. Excuses to retain him were falling short.

'Unless there is a significant reason for us to stay, we will have to leave tomorrow,' Sugreev confided sadly. I was becoming increasingly used to his friendship. The possibility of his departure was painful.

That evening, I found Anjani ma sitting with a pronounced frown on her face. I sat beside her.

'What is it, Tara?' she asked.

'I want to ask the same thing. What is it, and how can I help?'

'We need Bali and Sugreev. Bali doesn't want to stay here. Our leadership proposal has fallen flat,' she shook her head. 'The moment Bali is gone, Dunduvi will attack.'

This was not news to me. I sat quietly, contemplating as I dug my nails into the soil. A column of ants scuttled out. 'Let him go if he is so keen, we don't care.' I declared, though uncertainty clouded my heart.

'Really, Tara!' Anjani ma said angrily. 'Not that I haven't noticed your hostility towards Bali, for reasons I'm unaware of. Whatever may have happened between you two, could it be more important than the safety of the tribe?'

'It isn't,' I agreed. Women, especially mothers, tend to notice everything. 'I didn't ask him to leave.'

'You didn't ask him to stay either,' Anjani ma said. 'Why do you think he hasn't left yet? I suppose partly because of gratitude. He cares about us, but mainly because he wants to reconcile, I can tell.'

'He wouldn't throw a banana peel at me,' I

protested, crushing a leaf between my fingers. I had hurt him, although unintentionally. He had hurt me too. Neither of us had tried to make amends.

'Not everyone can bend. Some just brood. Wouldn't it be worth trying, Tara?' Anjani ma swayed to and fro, a wicked smile on her face. 'His heart lies with the younger one, who seems tied to your tail these days.' She handed me a banana and whispered, 'The other day, I caught Bali standing afar, staring at the datura beds. Who sighs for datura unless it's linked to a memory with ...?'

'What will I get in return?' I asked sweetly, having regained my footing.

She scratched my shoulder, irritation carved on her lips. 'I know your terms, Pishachini. A secret for a secret. You will have it.'

An expert negotiation after a long time, since the fight with Bali. I stood up, satisfied.

*

'Ask Bali what will make him stay back with us. The tribe wants him here,' I said carefully. 'Don't tell him this came from me. Just convince him. Can you do that for me?'

Sugreev gazed into the horizon in silence. 'What if he demands something the tribe agrees to give, but you don't?'

'The tribe needs him; I don't. If the tribe can afford his price, why should I object?' I stuck my tongue out at him. Sugreev walked away.

That evening, everyone had gathered on the grasslands at the fringes of the banana forest. Some were singing lullabies; others chattering away; many sat shivering; and the rest were dozing off. I relaxed on a tree branch, blankly staring at the moon, wondering what Bali's terms would be. Below, Ruma and my father were busy extracting juices from the wild flowers. Sugreev appeared, walking with broad strides. I don't know why, but my heart sank. Everyone crowded around him. I didn't move. Sugreev avoided looking at me.

'Bali will stay if Tara marries him!'

The trees in the forest forgot to breathe. After

a brief silence, everyone cheered loudly. My father joined the party with his tail high up in the air. Some ran to pluck the auspicious bananas. The celebratory fruit was distributed among all. Only Ruma stood alone, her banana fell to the ground.

I leapt off quietly, jumping from one branch to the other, moving far away from the tribe. My ears were burning. So Bali wanted to punish me for life? The tribe, those whom I called my own, were so blind as to not see this? Or did they see it and still not mind sacrificing one girl for everyone's security? What an enormous betrayal! I sat down, burying my head between my knees. I needed an exit plan at the earliest. I could run away, but isolating myself from the tribe would be foolish. Should I coax Ruma into telling me the recipe for poison? Or, forget that, how about crushing the datura and feeding an overwhelming quantity of the seeds to the elder twin? How much would be enough to induce brain death in the giant?

7

'I am sorry about Bali's death,' Sita said, startling me. Coincidentally, she stood at the very spot of the forest where Sugreev had once voiced Bali's proposal. I looked at her sharply and straightened myself.

'There is an insurmountable wall between Bali and me – one that neither of us can cross. But we are still together. Someday I will go back to the same Bali who lived, loved and laughed with me.' I inched closer to Sita and whispered, 'Have you come back to the same Ram you had left behind in Panchavati Forest?'

The wide-eyed woman had not expected such directness. Why should I mince my words for her comfort? She took a while to frame her response. 'What makes you think I didn't?'

Eh! The masquerading humans. I nodded sarcastically and let it go. Sita pushed further. 'You are talking about the fire test?'

I had no intention of explaining anything. Humans are too sensitive.

'When the fire of suspicion was lit, every eye was on me. They were eager to know if Sita would perish or sustain. No one bothered to trace Ram.' She smiled peacefully. 'Dense smoke meandered up from the plumes, blinding and choking those who doubted me.' Divine gratification spread over her face. 'I didn't walk through the fire alone; Ram was with me.' She turned to look at me. 'Else, he could have left me after the battle was won.'

I couldn't help staring in awe. Words escaped me, allegations dissolved. 'Why didn't you refuse the fire test, Sita?' I asked, jumping around her restlessly. 'You had the courage to stay firm before Ravan; why surrender now?'

'I did not surrender. I underwent the fire test to protect Ram,' she explained, shocking me again. Did she just say "protect"? How on earth did someone protect the powerful?

'After a long separation restricting obvious interactions, people wanted to know if I still loved Ram. Whether I was still partnering him and, through him, them? Or had the captive of Lanka been influenced by the charismatic enemy chief? If I had been proved unfaithful, people would also lose faith in Ram's power to love. They wanted reassurance; I only helped settle their doubts.'

I stood before her, scratching my head, wondering which one of us was mad. 'What if your people need proof again? And again. And again? Would you keep indulging them forever?'

'No, I wouldn't,' Sita promised. 'If distrust becomes their habit, I will pull in the reins.'

The trees above us swayed gently in the breeze. She asked me about Angad and Bali, and about a usual day in Kishkindha. I got her to reminisce her days in Mithila and Ayodhya. Leaning against each other, we fondly remembered our loved ones, until it was time for her to leave. I walked her to the base of Rishyamukh, from where she would journey ahead.

'I hope to see you again.' She turned to face me and held my hands between hers.

'I hope you never do,' I said, surprising her. 'May you always be sheltered within the riches of your castle. May you never have to step out into the wild again.'

Sita laughed. We hugged. And I returned to my desolate bed in the forest.

8

The forest was dark. The trees were stiff. Not a single leaf dared to stray. Rage surged through me as the sound of pounding footsteps drew nearer. Two strides ahead, a bamboo stick lay unevenly broken. Bears must have trampled and slit it, leaving jagged edges. I angled the pieces, aiming for the forehead, ankle and chest. They landed in the right places, oozing blood and imposing wounds. My face contorted into a thousand patterns. Seldom is anything more bitter than a deceiving friend.

Sugreev uttered not a single word. He accepted the punishment, his face bowed, waiting for my wrath to subside. I had picked up a handful of thorny bushes to hurl at him. But when I realized he wouldn't defend himself, I threw them away.

'What are you made of? Deadwood?' I cried furiously. He didn't move. 'How could you say that?' I wanted to pummel him or drown myself in the Pampa. 'You didn't feel it was important to tell me first?' His forbearance was more upsetting than Bali's insolence. 'Speak up! Answer me,' I hissed.

'I didn't think it through, Tara,' he said apologetically. 'Just relayed Bali's response to the offer made by the tribe.'

'Bali's response, Sugreev? Is he all that matters?' I backflipped. 'Does the time we spent together mean nothing? Was the camaraderie, our trust, as wobbly as a ginger shoot?' My tone had softened now, more dejected than angry. 'Do you have no responsibility towards me?'

He finally looked up. 'You are asking me, Tara? You fought with Bali. You vanished. Bali sought you out and brought you home. You refused to have Bali around. He respected that and commanded me to accompany you everywhere, lest you do something silly again ...'

Sugreev continued to ramble on, establishing God knows what. His last sentence had paralysed my thoughts. I felt trapped in a world that was no longer mine, where everything was being orchestrated by someone else, subtly enough for me to believe my choices mattered. Talking to Sugreev was futile – I would have to deal with Bali directly.

'Tell me something, Sugreev,' I spat out with great resentment. 'Why would someone in love with another woman want to marry me?'

'Not again, Tara,' The monkey glanced around in anguish, making sure no one was within earshot. I smirked sarcastically before turning away.

'Tara,' I heard him say as he leapt closer. 'Listen, for heaven's sake, don't start with this ever again. Bali could be in the kind of danger that the animal world knows nothing about.'

Shocked, I spun around to face him. Danger? My heart missed several beats.

'An imperious rogue has hidden her,' Sugreev hesitated. 'No one dares mention her name. She is infamous, a sinful enchantress. Dauntingly beautiful. She brings bad luck to those around her. We don't know if she is alive or dead. Bali must be kept away from anything related to her. Or, the rogue might come after him. You understand? Please, stop mentioning her.'

Who was *she*? What about this imperious rogue who had hidden her? Curiosity, like the chirrups of hooligan sparrows, flew in from everywhere. I pressed my lips together. My fight with Bali and everything that happened afterwards felt naive and overdramatic compared to this new thriller.

Quietly, I started walking back towards the tribe. Sugreev remained standing there. As I crossed a grove, the music grew louder. The tribe was playing tree trunks and singing happy songs; some were dancing as well. Even the trees had sacrificed their slumber, their branches shaking with frenzied elegance. Ginger juice on their roots! Ruma was nowhere to be seen. I stood in a corner, feeling hopeless about the unfolding events. Anjani ma whistled softly from the left side. She gestured for me to sit beside her, evidently pleased with whatever had transpired. My father, I was told, had gone to meet Bali after waiting for me long enough. I closed my eyes and prayed. 'Bhagwan, please slow down.' I felt like I was falling freely from the sky, with not a single branch to grab onto.

Anjani ma gently trailed her fingers up my bare back, affectionately stroking my head.

'Yes, girl, I remember my promise,' she said happily.

Promise! Oh, her secret. What would I do with it now?

'Hanuman was notoriously naughty in his childhood,' Anjani ma did not notice my lack of interest. 'There was a time when he unintentionally irked two senior gods. You know who?'

How could I know? I remained quiet.

'Surya and Indra,' she revealed. 'The little one

had been learning terrible skills from Vayu Dev, the wind god. Vayu loved him. Like a father, he indulged him. When Hanuman leapt forward, the wind god stopped blowing from that direction, offering him the least resistance. Rather, he propelled the boy in the direction of his flight from the back. During one such leap, Hanuman aimed to swallow the morning sun. He thought it was a fruit.'

The moonlight shone on our faces. I was being carefully observed by the talkative woman beside me. When would Father return? I looked eastwards.

'Surya forgave him, but not Devraj Indra,' Anjani ma continued. 'He was angry at the little monkey's audacious encroachment into the celestial systems. Hanuman was struck by the harrowing *vajra* on his chin. The young boy fell unconscious. He would have broken his head if Vayu hadn't caught him mid-air. Vayu threatened to withdraw air from the earth if Hanuman wasn't returned to life. That's how my beautiful child came back to my lap.' Anjani ma wiped her eyes.

'Since then, he is called Vayu Putra, to honour the god who breathed new life into a cursed body.'

Hanuman's deep mark on his chin was known to all. I prayed for his long life. Anjani ma spoke again. 'That day Vayu made me a promise. Indra would also suffer the pain he had once caused to me.' Anjani ma raised her hands to touch her forehead, bowing before the wind god.

'You want Indra punished?' I asked softly.

'No, I don't. Neither does Hanuman,' she said. 'I got back my child, and there ended that chapter.'

'Tell that to Vayu dev,' I uttered unmindfully. 'What's the point of getting Indra's child killed?'

'I don't want to settle any score. I don't want Indra's child killed. Believe me.' Anjani ma suddenly held my palm with extreme urgency. 'But the universe documents every karma and adjusts destiny to counter its effect. It is not for any of us to control.'

The elderly lady spoke as if Indra's child was a very important figure in my life. As if she was answerable to me. I smiled at her. Maybe old age brought her a strange sense of guilt. 'What would you do if Devraj Indra's child stood before you today?' I asked, hoping to divert her thoughts.

'I would protect him,' she said immediately. 'I would love him as much as I love my Hanuman ... Hanuman?' She suddenly exclaimed. I turned around.

Hanuman stood behind us, my father smiling beside him. Anjani ma kissed his forehead as my father did to me.

'Tara, I know Bali well. It will be impossible for you to not love him,' he whispered in my ears, hugging me like he used to when I was a child. 'Mark my words. Your dispute, whatever it is, will wither away.'

It was a sleepless night for all of us, though my reasons differed from those of the others.

*

The next morning, I waited near the Pampa at a time when Bali would typically return from his morning prayers. The lake quivered, rolled and whirled, the ripples shimmering between his large hands and legs. He tumbled forward and backward below the water surface, suddenly throwing his limbs straight down and shooting jets of water into the sky – his hands joined together with rare elegance. The energetic eyes looked tensed as he emerged from the water.

'I shouldn't have asked about *her*,' I said without any preamble.

His jaws tightened. 'Who told you?' he asked and turned away. 'Of course, who else.' He sat down, waiting for his body to dry.

'Why do you want to get married? You want to punish me?' My voice choked.

'Who can punish you, Tara? I tried once and have regretted it ever since.' He sounded nothing like the brute I had seen earlier. 'In order for me to gain citizenship of the forest – as your folk want me to – I cannot remain an outsider. Earning the love and trust of the animals can only be achieved through our marriage. The tribe owns you; your father is like a father to them.'

Oh, this was meant to be a political alliance. Commendable. I crossed my arms over my chest. 'Why do you even want to stay back? We mean nothing to you.'

Bali shook his head to disperse the water from his fur. A few droplets landed on my face. 'What I am searching for, I may never find. I've tried my best to not believe this.' The deep pain in his voice was unmistakable. Falling leaves of ketaki trees fluttered around us. 'Without this search, I am jobless. Without the job, I might go mad. The tribe has kindly conferred a task upon me. Sugreev wants to settle down here. Maybe I should too.'

No one could be impolite to a grieving heart. Bali stood up, perhaps waiting for me to disperse so he could get moving as well. 'Why not Ruma? I think she …'

'No, not Ruma. I can't. She reminds me of someone.' He spoke with his eyes closed, his mind lost elsewhere.

The heart tends to forgive those who need love. It also softens for those capable of giving love, regardless of who may be the fortunate beneficiary. I wanted to meet Ruma at the earliest; she had been hiding since the day before. But wait! Was Bali talking about *her*?

Bali raised his head to find me still standing, shocked. 'What?' he asked.

'You mentioned the secret. It is dangerous for you ...'

His expression shifted from astonishment to amusement, eventually breaking into silent laughter. 'I don't know if it's dangerous for me, but I'm sure I can handle any kind of danger. Please explain that to the idiot. And if possible, tell him not to feel scared of imaginary adversities.' He coughed twice, trying to clear his throat. 'This is not a subject I like to discuss. Its too personal.'

Would his wife be entitled to his personal secrets? I held back my thoughts. Where would Ruma be now, and what would she be doing? Talking to Bali had been of no use other than having melted my heart a little for him. I couldn't understand how to dodge the proposal while retaining the twins. What was I to do with a handsome creature whose seductive eyes searched for someone else?

I stuck my tongue out and slapped my head. Bali was neither handsome nor seductive – I reminded myself – there was no need to be overly kind towards a high-headed snob.

'There's something you should know.' He caught my wandering attention. 'Not every day in the forest was it Sugreev sitting with you.'

My hands and legs felt weak. How had I not guessed? 'Why, Bali? On all those days when Sugreev was oddly silent, it was actually you?' I flared up. 'This is unfair.'

Bali sounded remorseful. 'I wanted to apologize. I wanted to talk. Each time I held back because ...'

'Because?' I insisted, visibly upset.

'Being nice to you would make it difficult for me to leave,' he said with a straight face, turning towards the Pampa. 'And now, if I am to stay, then my motivation is quite clear.'

'Stay here or leave, for all I care. You foolish, ginger-mouthed chatter-bug,' I lashed out obstinately and started to walk away with a grimace. 'If you get nasty, I'll slit your head.'

He leapt forward and stood before me. 'Claim me as yours, Tara; I will do anything to make you happy.' His eyes shone. 'I will turn this place into a magnificent kingdom for animals. A sanctuary of abundance and security. Brains will be trained for acuity. Bodies will be trained to execute the vision of the brain. A jungle where trees feel loved, travellers find shade, miscreants face prosecution. Your land, your terms.'

Not Bali's dream. He was letting go of his chase for the benefit of others. This giving was noble. It should be received by someone more deserving. I leapt past him.

'Where is Ruma?' I asked everyone. No one knew, no one seemed bothered.

'What about her?' Anjani ma chided when she saw me freaking out. 'If she's not here, she's out doing something important. She's an obedient girl. Not compulsively reckless like you.'

I nodded sadly. Obedience, like disobedience, has no rewards – only discreet punishments. I climbed a nearby tree. The woodland lowered some of its branches, exposing the other side of the terrain beyond the Pampa Sarovar. She was busy picking fallen fruits. I joined her in collecting the produce.

She smiled. 'Why this sudden benevolence?' I didn't answer. 'I am happy for you, Tara,' she said finally, making it easy for me to talk.

'Why don't you speak out?' I threw down the fruit from my hand and hugged her. 'If you don't want to, I can.'

'Don't!' she warned, pulling me into an embrace. 'Like the many secrets you hoard, let my infatuation for Bali remain locked within your wicked ribs,' she said pensively. 'When stories fall into the wrong ears, they get misconstrued. No one understands despair; they only humiliate.'

'Why live with despair? Fight it.' I pushed her and she rolled away.

'Pishachini!' she rebuked. 'Remember the datura? It has medicinal properties. The plant can be poisonous too. Bali is also an intoxicant. Cannot be misused. At least I won't.'

'Love is not misuse,' I argued. 'I carry red chillies for him in my heart.'

'That suits the future king,' she countered. 'I'll have expectations. You won't.'

9

'Bali. Bali. Bali!' I called out until he heard.

'What, woman!' he answered finally. 'Has the tribe thrown you out of the land?'

'Would you have married Ruma, had she asked you to?' I asked bluntly.

'Why do you have to repeatedly dredge up the haunted pages of history?' He sounded as if he had been pulled out of a long-delayed slumber.

'Because they tell me more about you. Now speak,' I insisted.

'You are so childish,' he openly disapproved; but disapprovals strengthened my resolve. He was well aware of that. 'Who told you she didn't?'

His words hit me like a falling melon. 'She didn't what?'

'Ask me to marry her,' he said, as if he was talking about a change of seasons.

'When?' I felt devastated. 'You both kept this hidden from me?'

'Why hide, Tara? It was irrelevant.' Bali did not understand my plight. 'She was your friend. For me, she was this girl who was just always there, making things available before being asked. Sweet.'

'Affection does not matter to you?' I asked softly.

'She came to me the day before Sugreev approached the tribe with the proposal of our marriage,' he admitted, ignoring my question. 'I suggested she marry Sugreev instead. Sugreev was capable of loving anyone who had my approval. I was a miser – an amateur in love yet arrogantly selective.'

10

An amateur in love yet arrogantly selective. Only Bali could have said something like this. He was a man of words, though. The forest became his dedicated project. He pushed the boundaries, never happy with any less. Effortlessly, he tuned into the discomforts of the animals, devising solutions no one had thought of before. Nal and Nil, our mischievous neighbours, no longer dropped the tribe's belongings into the Pampa. Bali introduced them to shells of fruits that floated on the water. He trained them to jump higher with each spring. They were overjoyed, thinking they had finally acquired supremacy over water and air, both. The great bear was delighted at the discoveries of the new and tasty edibles. Sugreev brought the samples to Ruma. She evaluated their suitability for animal consumption. Jambavan volunteered as Ruma's tester, nibbling on leaves, shoots, roots and god know what! He dispersed the selected seeds for further growth. The idle slopes of Rishyamukh were assigned to cultivate the plants that secreted medicinal juices under Father's supervision.

Anjani ma and Uncle Kesari had found their lost child in Bali. They were moved to tears when he sat with them for hours, getting them to brag about Hanuman's legendary adventures. Earlier, they would lament that Hanuman would have solved any problem with a flick of his fingers if he were not travelling. Now, they pointed to Bali for solutions ranging from the lack of rainfall to decrease in mango buds. Strangely, at the peak of summer, when the ground cracked and the grasslands dried up, Bali would stand under the open sky with his arms stretched out, praying for rains. The black clouds would rush in to cover the sky immediately, clashing against each other in haste, thundering between the lightning. And it rained!

'How does he do this?' I asked Sugreev.

My meetings with Sugreev had reduced considerably. He didn't come to me too often now. Off and on we bumped into each other. He greeted and moved on, I lagged behind with a frown. One day I managed to hop before him.

'Do I look like a moron who will share any information with you?' He leapt backward.

'How moronic you look, we will discuss in detail on some other day. But what's the problem?'

'Stay away from me, mad woman,' he scowled. 'You pick up confidential information only to divulge it at the wrong places, completely out of turn. I have to bear the brunt of the biggie.'

'Me!' I was shocked. 'What information of yours did I divulge?'

'Oh, really? One fine morning, Bali must have dreamt of me telling you about the danger concerning *her*. You blabbermouth! Go, mind your own tail.'

'I did not say anything,' I tried to make peace. 'Your brother is over smart.'

Sugreev was not convinced, nor pleased. He moved away in broad steps. How much I missed Sugreev's banter and his inputs on my script. I couldn't stop him to convey that. Ruma emerged from the other end of the grove. They exchanged something, and Ruma's head dropped to his shoulders. Sugreev rubbed his ear against her head. She chuckled. He lifted her in his arms and disappeared into the forest.

*

Ruma was unusually quiet until the morning of our wedding. She had informed Anjani ma that she wanted to marry Sugreev. He looked at Bali and received an affirmation. Hanuman had been especially summoned that evening. He was to coronate Bali as the king of the hinterland. He brought along two large maces. The younger monkey couldn't lift his gift, Bali juggled them over his head. Everyone cheered and distributed bananas.

'Bali, what would you like to name your kingdom?' Hanuman asked with a smile.

'What is the need for a name, brother?' Bali countered. 'Names are limiting. Till date everyone has survived with the forest just being the forest. Why do we need one now?'

'You are right,' Hanuman remained reticent. 'But limits are important.'

Bali was about to respond when Jambavan entered, shouting and abusing in pain. Blisters were spread all over his face and body. All attention shifted there. The bear had raided a beehive again to fill himself with the honey and came back with nasty stings. Serious discussions went for a toss. Bali wheeled away to hide a giggle and Hanuman sat tapping his forehead. Ruma rushed to help the suffering animal.

'So, what is going on here?' Jambavan asked once he felt better. He had forgotten about the weddings.

'They couldn't decide whether they should name the place,' Ruma said calmly.

'What do you suggest? Every place should have a name, no?' I barged in. 'Why should we call it a forest? Every forest is a forest.'

Bali glanced at me, so did Ruma. Usually his greatest supporter, Ruma echoed, 'The new king doesn't want a name. Hanuman insists there should be one.'

In the meanwhile, I quietly went behind Jambavan. The honeycomb was lying near his left hand.

'Name for this place, eh! Of course, this place has a name.' Jambavan smiled innocently. 'Kishkindha. When I was younger, I called the forest Kishkindha. Why this weird name? Because the forest was weird! See, the tamal trees wouldn't object when these silly monkeys climbed them. So I tried once. Now don't ask me what happened next. Such an embarrassing story, he he he he … Hey!' I was met with an angry scowl when the soft leaves touched his blisters. 'You girls stole my honey?' he screamed.

'Do you realize how much effort it took me to extract? These foolish women are applying to my face what should be delightfully devoured? How could you?'

'Be quiet,' Ruma reprimanded. 'We have only taken a swipe. Honey will bring down the swelling and relieve the pain. You can rest now. I'd like to proceed with my wedding.'

Having scolded, Jambavan suddenly lost his vigour. He sat grumbling, unhappy at the misuse of his treasure. I handed the honeycomb back to him. He lifted it to pour some honey into his mouth.

'Kishkindha!' The proclamation startled him and everyone else. The contents from the honeycomb clumsily dropped over Jambavan's neck and shoulder. He was aghast. His culprit paid no heed. 'Jambavan has decided the name. This place will henceforth be called Kishkindha. Even the tiger will have to think twice before entering the land of the monkeys and bears. Let us unite for Kishkindha.'

A hush fell over everyone. Jambavan was yet to understand what had transpired. Sugreev shifted uncomfortably in his place. Ruma slapped my arm. Hanuman turned towards Bali. I looked on expectantly.

'Even the tiger will have to think twice before entering the land of the monkeys and bears. Unite for Kishkindha,' Bali repeated. The crowd erupted in cheer. Good wishes for a beautiful, robust dream called Kishkindha emerged from the earthlings, spreading sidewards and upwards amid euphoric happiness. Jambavan, forgetting his pains, started singing a song – funny and joyful, fantasizing unlimited food, sleep and friends. The monkeys danced around, repeating him in chorus. Separated by the grooving blokes with the great bear in between, Bali and I locked eyes as much as we tried to tear ourselves away from each other.

In the animal world, this wedding thing is not a formal ritual. It is just a sense of belonging between two souls. A consensual choice to remain together, standing by each other through storms and quakes. Not that unwilling bodies are not forced. It happened often. But we are free to love. The need of our bodies merge with the romance in our minds. We feel married; we do not really get married. That evening, I felt married to Bali. A casual conversation to distract the old bear had exposed his childhood memories. Bali won hearts with one single stroke. Valuing emotions of others over opinions of self was the feat of a nice man with a soft heart camouflaged inside a tough body. I had to acquire that secret heart.

*

Hanuman came soon and dragged Bali away with a hand on his shoulder. I turned to Ruma. 'What is happening there?'

'They have plans to go fishing,' she said, equally peeved. I planted a soft kick on the back of her leg. She fell to the ground. 'The elders will formally induct him into the geography of Kishkindha and its surroundings, as well as any cultural practices that he is unfamiliar with. He will also be introduced to the possible dangers around, their paths and the usual characters of attack.'

I glanced at Bali, who was following Hanuman without any complaint. He didn't look back. 'Whose idea was this?'

'Anjani ma, who else,' Ruma said with disgust. '*Bali must know, and Sugreev must listen,*' she imitated the old lady.

I chuckled. 'She has a point. The one who takes a round of the world every morning must be introduced to the north and south of Kishkindha.'

'I had reminded them too. But you know how the elders are.' Ruma folded her knees, burying her chin in between. 'They will tell you everything you know as if you don't know anything, and then they'll tell everyone that if they hadn't told, you wouldn't have known.' She looked at me. 'In case you are hoping for anything exciting this night, please splash the water of Pampa over it and go to sleep.'

'Shut up, pervert.' I slapped her.

'Pervert? Me? You were shamelessly gawking at Bali with some spiritual appetite?' She pushed me but inched closer as well. 'Hey, you think the brothers would be thinking about us while listening to the doctrines?'

'Without a doubt,' I affirmed. 'Though it's unlikely for them to converse the way we are doing. Sugreev would be restless, his boring elder brother silent, and Uncle Kesari endlessly talkative.'

The monkeys were still dancing ahead of us. *Keep quiet and let me think,* I wanted to scream. True wisdom comes from contemplation. But sacrilegious ideas are born in the spur of the moment. Slowly, I turned to Ruma and Ruma towards me.

Soon, some monkeys were picked from the carnival. Coconut water was distributed, with instructions to feed the seniors first. The new king of the terrain had arranged for refreshments. Each monkey received a symbolic welcome to Bali's kingdom. Only the king and his brother were made to wait until the others had their share. Sugreev wore an expression of deep dissatisfaction on his face; his coconut was missing. Others had drank their fill and started devouring the flesh. Conversations lulled into drowsy murmurs, until they fell asleep upon each other.

Bali got up. 'Come,' he called out to Sugreev.

'I won't,' Sugreev sulked. 'They did not keep coconuts for us.'

'Very well, then,' Bali shrugged. 'Wait till Ruma gets here and turns you into a coconut.'

When Ruma saw Bali returning alone, she smacked her head with the back of her hand. 'Buffoon, he has no clue. I'll go fetch him.' With that, she rose. I wasn't sure if she left or remained by my side. I watched Bali walking forward, naughty smiles playing on his face.

'What did you put in the coconut?' He scratched his head.

'Datura,' I admitted, nervously biting my nails.

He lifted his hand to stifle his laughter. 'What if you are caught tomorrow?'

'It was the king's treat; I was merely catering,' I leapt away, prompting him to follow. We left behind the towering trees and entered the palmyra orchard, the cylindrical trunks peeking into the sky. I stopped abruptly at a spot where the moon shone the brightest. Bali was brought to a sudden halt as my back slammed against his chest. The unfamiliar nervousness manifested beads of perspiration on his forehead and arms. Hesitantly, he placed his palms gently on my shoulders. When I didn't protest, he lowered his head to my neck, his hands encircling my waist. My hands fell upon his, hugging both him and myself. The passing breeze ruffled my fur. The wildflowers showered us with their gift of fragrance.

'You really didn't want a name for the place?' I asked out of the blue.

'Until the time we advance ahead without being questioned, we claim the land as ours.' It wasn't the most appropriate topic for the hour, but he didn't shut me off.

'You mean the world is ours as long as we are not stopped?' I cocked my head.

He chuckled. 'Precisely. Boundaries are for the stupid humans.'

'And when we are stopped? Do we fight?' I gazed up at the moon.

Bali brushed my cheek with his, I closed my eyes. The touch was rough yet gentle. 'We don't seize anything from anyone. Not if it is rationally owned or rightfully possessed over time. Fighting costs life. We can make friends instead. Maybe even share resources in times of need.'

'Then why did you agree to put a name to your kingdom?' I turned towards him, listening to the loud thuds of his heart.

Bali lifted my chin with his fingers, looking into my eyes. 'Because you wished it. Your honour is mine too. Your decision holds.'

My hands wrapped around his neck now, our lips grazing each other's. 'You wouldn't stop me if I gave orders?'

'Never. You know better,' he promised. 'But I will question your decisions.' He tugged my leg, and I slipped. Bali's arms wrapped themselves around me before I hit the ground. He drew me closer to his chest. Not an inch of my body was spared from the pleasure. I moaned, quivered and whimpered. On our wedding night, he bestowed on me a rare gift – the intimate secrets of our bodies!

11

How beautiful were those days when I could tease Bali whenever I wished. He would be watching the saras, herons and cranes loitering on the banks of the Pampa. I would stand at a distance, one hand suggestively gripping my waist, whistling at a pretty swan in the water, praising its red lips, advising it to spread its legs well while swimming. After pretending not to understand the carnal innuendos for a long while, Bali would suddenly get up and chase me. I would sprint as fast as I could, amid squeals of laughter, darting behind a tree and scrambling up another. Bali would catch me eventually, and we'd roll on the ground. He'd crush me between his arms. No mercy.

At one end of the forest, the ashwagandha was growing well. It needed a mix of red soil and sand to prevent waterlogging. Red flowers of vanjula also raised their heads near the Pampa. The knowledge for cultivating these were gleaned long ago from the chakravak birds. Seeds were unavailable. After our marriage, these were Bali's first gifts to me. He knew exactly where to find the vanjula. I passed them on to Ruma, who stocked samples of the plants in her laboratory at the palmyra garden. Their large, pointed leaves were used for storage and transfer of ingredients during her experiments. Barring my father, Ruma demanded complete privacy. Bali obeyed. Sugreev grumbled. I promised to infringe the day I felt inclined to do so.

One of those nights, he led me to an untrodden part of the forest. I was sure this corner did not exist before. It bore a mysterious aura imbued by the divine in the middle of dense woods. *Drawa, champaca, karnikara* and other flowers blossomed generously here in shades of red, violet and yellow.

Their fragrance could arouse the impassive; troubles of the hustled would suspend into a trance. Unknown birds with melodious voices sang of their union. Their songs illustrated lush imagery of broad leaves, thick trunks and dew-kissed soil carpeted with soft grass.

In the mornings, before sunrise, Bali would get up to commence his prayers on the bank of the Pampa. I would hold him by the arm and pull him back to me.

'Let me go, woman. Time is flying,' he tried to push me away, but ended up brushing my ear with his mouth instead. When I remained passive, he grew irritated. 'What?'

'Why do you circle the world every morning?' I blew air over his nose.

He took a moment to respond. 'That's how I worship Mother Earth. Is there a problem?'

'Just that? Those who don't make rounds don't worship?' I caressed his shoulder.

He laughed before getting up, freeing himself. 'Tara, you seek secrets in everything. Relax.'

'Usually, there is indeed a secret in everything,' I shot back, still reclining lazily on the bed of leaves. I sensed that my words had made Bali uncomfortable.

'Every secret of my body, you know. How to soothe, when to go slow, what to pursue and where to withdraw. What else do you seek, queen of desire?' he whispered, his breath heavy. I said nothing. He pulled out the leaves clinging to his fur and tossed them at me before setting off.

'Will you take me with you? Around the world?' I called out from behind.

This irked Bali. He didn't like to be stopped after he had started moving. He didn't answer, nor did he turn to acknowledge my question.

I stood up quickly to gather mud, rocks and leaves from the ground, moulding them into a large sphere. I rolled it ahead. Just before the ball could hit Bali, he gave it a rear kick, sending it rolling back towards me. I fled.

*

When the cuckoo filled the air with the songs of spring, I tried to sing along. The haughty bird preferred to perform solo. After a few moments of silence, it sang again. I followed suit. It stopped again. The game continued. My script needed designs to symbolize more sounds. But the ones I was creating looked bad. The simpler ones were already exhausted. I wanted to pelt caterpillars at Sugreev for ditching our brainstorming midway. I would have pursued him had the cuckoo not resumed singing. I mimicked its music.

'No work other than troubling poor things?'

I spun around. I hadn't noticed Bali approaching from behind. He had spent the morning with the young monkeys, teaching them about the discipline of ants and the unity of birds. He had tasked them with surveying how reptiles intimidated their foes before reconvening in the evening.

'How did the monkey king manage to slip past the royal guards in broad daylight?' The expression on the face in front was of amusement, the kind that could irk even the most saintly being on the earth. No answer to my question.

'Where do you keep Sugreev occupied these days? Why doesn't he talk to me?' I asked, partly to address my curiosity and partly to wipe that irritating expression off his face.

'Me!' Thankfully, something like a response emerged. 'I have no hand in this. He must be attending to something productive.'

I narrowed my eyes at the implication of the last sentence. 'What brings you here?' This was the time when Bali would be with the tribe, listening to the tales of yore, learning about life in the land before our generation was born. Memories of the elders were music for him. He would personally visit the sites where our ancestral impressions had been immortalized. If there was anything that could pluck him away from those branches, it certainly wasn't romance.

'I am told that you know what is happening in various parts of the world. How?'

Eh, that's business! 'My secret,' I replied coyly, sensing frustration building in him.

'What nonsense, Tara!' he exclaimed. 'You know how important it is for us to …' he stopped, gauging that logic would not suffice. 'Fine, what is it you want in return?'

'It's always the same,' I said indifferently. 'A secret for a secret.'

'What secret of mine do I have to offer to my wife?' he blurted out, his irritation thinly masked.

'I will ask when the time comes. You will have to answer then,' I replied, feeling my heart crumble like the dust of broken leaves. The trees around spying on every conversation dropped rotten flowers, prompting me to release the words locked inside my heart. But I couldn't muster the courage to bring it up again. I didn't want to hurt him. I didn't want him to hurt me. Situations may have changed, but memories hadn't.

Bali seemed fine with this arrangement. He waited expectantly.

'The birds tell me. The bees, too. They discuss among themselves, and I eavesdrop.' I smiled sheepishly. 'For each secret of theirs, I share one of mine.'

Bali didn't smile; he could not speak for a while. Instead, he jumped around restlessly. 'You know, Tara, this is who we are,' he urged passionately. 'Animal instincts are traditionally attuned to share their strengths and cohabitate. More we evolve towards the human race, the more our senses dull.'

As much as I liked Bali's spirit, his loyalty to the wild remained beyond my grasp. I had heard his arguments with Sugreev, which the younger twin could never win, yet he persevered. Sugreev wanted to discipline the forest. But Bali would not let anyone touch the forest. He wanted others to discipline themselves according to the will of the forest. Sugreev advocated introducing tools that reduced physical labour. Bali opposed vehemently. 'Don't rationalize laziness. Use your body, fool. Practise jumping higher and running faster – you will not need a chariot. It will make you stronger. You will need to sleep less, but you will sleep well,' he made a ruthless jest at his poor twin's fondness for slumber.

Even worse, he had Ruma's overt support. 'Underactive muscles slow down the digestion, resulting in tiredness, weight gain and depression.'

Sugreev was silenced for good. The elder twin would leave the couple alone, grumbling that monkeys did not need to ape humans, as animal virtues were far superior. Ruma would sit behind Sugreev, massaging his tail with the oils she had prepared. The tails of the twins were too bare. Sugreev would slap his tail on her neck and shoulders before she caught hold of it with both hands, pressing her feet on his back for balance. Bali did not allow anyone to touch his tail, not even me. I tried once again now. He dodged it, his eyes still filled with awe.

'You value originality and exclusivity. That pride is inspiring,' I tried to explain. 'Sugreev isn't against you; he is just cautious. Why do you resist change? Let's seek a common ground which blends traditional wisdom with modern evaluations?' I sincerely believed in fusion. Bali didn't.

'It's a wonderful theory, but ineffective in practice,' he remarked thoughtfully. 'We need to make a choice and stick to it. Otherwise, the confusion resulting from fusion will destroy everything.' He quickly changed the topic, bringing me back to the birds and the bees. 'So you understand their languages?'

'Yes, I do.' I admitted. 'I can even speak their language.' Feeling a bit shy, I looked away. His gaze was intense. He sat down, his arms touching mine. It wouldn't take too long for them to girdle my neck. The cuckoo began to sing as loudly as it could. This time, I couldn't sing alongside her.

'How do you know?' Bali asked, rubbing his nose tip against the side of my forehead. I didn't respond. One secret at a time. He didn't press further. His hand had barely touched my neck when a distant voice pierced the air.

'Baliiiiiiii,' Nal dragged out the name as long as he could. 'Where are youuuuuu? Come faaaaaaast. There is a crocodile in the Pampaaaaa.'

Bali leapt up and dashed away, transitioning from sensual to dutiful within the blink of an eye. The nasty owls broke into a noisy laughter. I charged from behind. 'Why don't you offer Nal's brain to it? Once the crocodile chews through his dry roughage, it will realize there's nothing for it in this land.'

Bali stopped and turned, laughing. 'Wicked.'

Nal continued progressing northwards, shouting, 'Anjani maaaaaaaa.' With the crocodile problem taken care of, he would undoubtedly fill her with complaints about me. I picked up a pebble and threw it in his direction.

'Hey! Listen,' I called out.

'Why do you do this?' Bali stopped, irritated at being called again from behind.

I chuckled. 'Will you teach me to fly? Like

your long leaps? I want to join you in the mornings,' I pleaded.

'If you want to leap with me, I will make it happen. Now don't call from behind again. I will send Sugreev.' He disappeared.

12

'Bali, did you kill the crocodile that day?'

'No, Tara, why should I?' his voice floated in. 'It was a small, bewildered creature that had lost its path and ended up there by swimming along the bottom of the lake. When it got tired, it climbed onto the bank to rest in the sun.'

'What did you do then? How did it go?' I had heard a distinct sound that evening. A strange noise, lingering like the beats of drums. I thought Bali must have smashed its head; the monkeys looked relieved.

'I was gently striking a rock with the mace,' he recalled. 'Crocodiles get stressed by low-frequency vibrations. The sound affects them. They fear danger approaching. This one quickly jumped back into the water and fled.'

'How do you know this, Bali?' I asked, surprised that an animal from the land would know such intricate details about another from the water.

'In Kishkindha, I learnt sustenance. Before I reached there, I learnt survival.'

I kept quiet. Time and again, I reached the threshold of the same closed gate which Bali didn't want to open and I didn't want to push.

'Why were you weeping the other morning, after I flew you across the world?'

I concentrated on counting the pollens of a wildflower. What would I say? That I was overwhelmed by the diversity of the world? That I was moved by Bali's unwavering care that never made me feel insignificant? That I was touched by his relentless pursuit, devoid of seeking support from a single other soul? Bali had silently compromised with his mission. That compromise was named Tara! I had wept bitterly, burying my head into his chest. He held me in a comforting embrace, softly patting my head with his palm.

'Why do you ask now?' Tears welled up in my eyes once more.

'If I asked then, you wouldn't have told me the truth.' His voice sounded sombre. *Did he miss holding me in his arms? Did our touch matter any longer, on the other side? I coughed, clearing my throat.*

'The one you searched for every single day, Bali, might one day come looking for you,' I said, feeling a pang of jealousy in my heart. 'What would you want me to tell her?'

An invisible sigh rustled through the stagnant leaves of the summer afternoon. 'Nothing,' he said. 'She'd know as much as you do – that Bali never stopped trying.'

13

That morning, I had accompanied Bali to the Pampa. He first worshipped his mace and then the earth. Next, he worshipped the sky. As he took the leap, he invited me to climb onto his back. Before I realized it, the wind came crushing down upon me. Bali had taken flight. It was terrifying. I clutched his body, my fingers gripping his shoulders. Everything I had grown up around was becoming smaller. The trees, the lake and the hills shrank. The sky widened.

I girdled him with my tail. Bali flew at a furious speed through the clouds, swerving right and left to avoid collisions. Below us, humans and animals were mere moving dots. I feared the wind might tear me away from Bali and fling me elsewhere, never to see the tribe again. Maybe my head would be smashed, or my backbone broken. Or I would drown in the sea. His tail curled around me, tying me firmly to his back. Now he flew even faster. Mountains and seas, deserts and ice lands appeared and disappeared below. My hands relaxed from encircling Bali's neck like an insecure snake.

My suspicion was not baseless.

Bali would fly very high above and suddenly dive as if he were about to land. But he would not. He would soar again, all the while searching for something. Something very important. Something very dear. Each time he expected to find a clue and tried to take a closer look, he was left disappointed. He would grunt in frustration and rise back to the clouds. Bali's journeys around the world were not merely his efforts to please Mother Earth. There was way more to it. By the time he landed at the base of Rishyamukh, his shoulder was wet with my tears.

*

With Sugreev's help, my script was progressing rapidly. We didn't restrict ourselves to the sounds of monkeys alone. We also noted down many sounds of other animals that were closer to ours, words that we felt would eventually evolve to be adopted into the colloquial monkey dialect. We made a list for those kinds. Symbolic expressions were borrowed from the various elements of nature. The taper of the fish and the curve of the mango, the bend of the banana and the round of the coconut, the crisscross of veins on the leaves and the shape of the petals were all tweaked to fit alphabetical iconography. We jumped with joy. However, Bali remained aloof.

'Don't ask me. Biggie has his own logic. Other than him, everyone else is a fool,' Sugreev complained.

'You both fought again,' I guessed. But 'fought' was the wrong word. Sugreev suggested alternatives, though never with conviction. Bali would dismiss them most of the times. He would then sulk in a corner until Ruma or I pulled him out with some excuse or the other.

'Look, I had offered the topmost branch of the tallest mango tree to be declared as the throne of Kishkindha. The bed of bananas lies on its right, which should be the king's private palace,' Sugreev explained. 'It is like that everywhere. The kings have their dedicated throne and courtroom, and a private abode with guards outside. But ...'

I didn't have to listen more. Even the banana plant dropped a cluster of ripe fruits, laughing at the counsel. The brothers had travelled for years and seen much. Sugreev wanted to organize things akin to humans, whom he believed to be more evolved. Bali detested his brother's tendency to imitate humans without considering the possible repercussions.

'Sugreev, do you really think that Bali is the kind to sit on top of a tree with a crown on his head?' I couldn't help blurting out. 'It is obvious that he wouldn't agree. Bali loves to be wherever he is needed.'

'If he doesn't, then why would the tribe continue to consider him the king? Identity doesn't create itself,' he frowned.

'True that,' I agreed. 'Identity needs to be cultivated authentically, not through a sense of superiority. One must be genuinely superior. Try to understand who our king truly is.'

'Fine then,' Sugreev replied, returning to his sulking.

That night, Bali returned late. I heard him leaping from branch to branch, searching for me. I was sitting quietly in the dark, leaning on the hay stacked inside the coconut grove interspersed with pineapple plants. The air was heavy with the strong fragrance of pineapples. Bali kept looking throughout the forest until he finally spotted me and crashed down beside. After a few moments of silence, smack! His tail spanked my head. 'Why did you make me wander?' he accused.

I slapped him back with mine. 'Because you kept me waiting.'

'Tara!' He exclaimed as he sat up angrily. 'I was at Rishyamukh. There could be a landslide next monsoon. The mountain is facing the sun directly, casting Kishkindha into its shade. The huge buddy is exhausted. I was there inspecting the situation. Before the rains arrive, we will have to restrict some of the slopes as unsuitable for animal adventures.'

I drew closer to him and lifted his hand to encircle my neck, while passing the pineapples picked for him. He took a large bite and put some slices inside my mouth. The juice spilled from my lips, trickling down the chin. He wiped them off. The poor monkey must not have eaten food for a very long time. He gobbled down the uneven pieces almost without chewing. I nestled closer to his chest.

'Bali, I think you should start utilizing monkey-power more effectively,' I said, tapping his arm.

Still chewing, he gestured with his hand and pronounced something weird through his full mouth, seeking to know more.

'You should not be the only one here, running around trying to solve every issue. Please delegate.'

'Delegate to whom?' he asked, taking another large bite. 'Sugreev is capable, but he can't handle pressure. I have tried everything – rebuking him, ridiculing him, explaining to him, even cajoling him. He is impossible. I can't trust him because he doesn't trust himself.'

'Not just Sugreev. All of us,' I stopped his rant. 'Me and Ruma. Nal and Nil. Jambavan. My father. Uncle Kesari and Anjani ma. Even Hanuman. It can't be that if problems come up from three different corners, then only one can be addressed because the king can't be in three places at the same time.'

Bali stopped munching. 'Fine, then. Delegating right now. Tell me the solution, not the problem.'

Well! I rolled my eyes. The monkey was getting smarter by the day. 'Think of the areas which need regular surveillance. Let the people help you. Let us build the next line of leadership.'

Soft smiles contoured Bali's face. He looked the best when he did this – a spontaneous, genuine grin coming straight from the heart. 'Ruma travels throughout the forest every day. She can educate the animals on quick-aides for common diseases and basic fitness. Everyone goes to Father for therapy; he can gather information on what is happening with whom and where. Hanuman is intuitive; he can meet the children from time to time, informing us of their maturing insights and unique talents. Uncle Kesari is always available to keep track of difficult terrains leading to injuries and accidents. He will work closely with you and Ruma. No one can handle the inter-tribe issues better than Anjani ma – she knows when to use the stick and how to reward. Nal and Nil can deal with engineering problems like the loose rocks of Rishyamukh. Jambavan can help with food collection; don't trust him for restoration, though! Divide the other monkeys into these groups so each leader can work with a team. And …'

I stopped wondering how receptive Bali would be to the proposal I was going to make. 'Teach me how to wield the mace. I'll need my team, too.'

Surprised, Bali lifted my face towards his. 'Are you sure?' he asked.

'When you go on your daily morning tour, I try to lift the mace. After days of practice, I lifted it to my chest today.' I bent my elbow and showed off the growing muscles in my arm.

The hazel eyes stilled. 'You are planning to render me jobless.'

'Not jobless, free!' I quipped. 'Only to ensure that a husband dedicates more time to himself and his wife.'

By now, Bali had finished the pineapples. He still looked hungry. So I passed him the coconuts.

'Our lazy lumps should assume responsibilities. Otherwise, they are too happy being cared for,' I contemplated. 'The monkeys can't continue to loiter aimlessly; they must show up as Bali's forces.'

'Okay, show me.' My husband suddenly started pressing on my head and tapping here and there. Surprised and irritated, I pushed him away. 'What?' he teased. 'Just checking which part of your head sprouts such explosive ideas.'

I kissed his forehead. 'Just little things a wife can do for the crownless king of the land.'

'My wife is my crown,' Bali murmured.

*

A few months later, when Bali had travelled to the bank of the Narmada River for his few days of penance, the passing birds informed that a large army was marching towards us and would reach us by the next morning. I rushed towards the tribe. Sugreev was tensed, Hanuman absent. I called upon the monkeys and prepared them for the upcoming situation.

'Bali would not approve of war,' I reasoned. 'Sugreev, we have to find a way to distract them.'

'If they are coming for blood, Tara, there is little we can do.' Sugreev trembled. 'Hope Bali returns at the earliest,' he began to pray, I grimaced.

An army that prided itself as the Asur troop reached us in the turn of a day, led by Ravan, the king of Lanka. We didn't have to do much. Ravan considered it beneath his dignity to fight with the monkeys. He had heard about Bali's impossible power and wanted to duel with him. Sugreev sent him away, saying that Bali was off on a pilgrimage. Ravan left to find him, while his soldiers camped on the outskirts of Kishkindha.

By the time Bali returned, he and Ravan had become close friends. I frowned, Sugreev sulked, the tribe was astonished. Bali called for celebrations. For the first time, Kishkindha welcomed foreign guests. During their conversations, I heard Ravan's angst against Indra.

'Who is this Indra?' I asked Bali when he finally had a moment amid the bed of banana trees.

'The king of the devas. Brings water to the earth. And controls the impulse of all living beings,' he explained reluctantly, making me sit up. 'My father.'

'Your father! Ravan was talking about Devraj Indra?' I exclaimed. I thought the twins were orphans. 'You never told me,' I accused.

'You never asked,' Bali snapped back. My nose flared with anger.

'Is this something to be asked? Or should it be disclosed during introductions. Duffer,' I chattered. 'Neither you nor Sugreev told us about your celestial lineage.'

'Sugreev is the son of Surya – the sun god.' Bali looked at my confused face. His words sounded like a mysterious, multi-layered riddle. I had started feeling very uncomfortable suddenly, remembering Anjani ma's story – the curse of Vayu dev for Indra's son. My head felt like over-chewed cud. The curse couldn't be about Bali, I reassured myself. But I needed to be very careful for the crazy twin. Well, one mystery at a time.

'You befriended your father's enemy?'

'Animals don't judge,' he mentioned coolly, munching on a banana.

'What made you bring him to Kishkindha?' I passed him another – a ripe one.

'He is knowledgeable. Enchanting. Entrancing.'

'How do you know?'

'Even the winds paused to hear Ravan reciting the *Shiva Stotra*. It was melodious, beautiful, captivating.'

I held him by the elbow from behind as he got up to leave. 'World's greatest liar, you said you didn't know he was locked between the folds of your tail,' I whispered. 'Then how did you hear his Shiva Stotra?'

'I didn't hear. I didn't say anything about hearing it.' He pulled me towards himself suddenly. An insect was crawling up his chin. I swiftly flicked it aside. 'You hallucinate too much. And talk too much.' Bali pushed me.

I fell to the ground. As he ran to save himself, I struggled to get back to my feet, my arm bruised by the edge of a rock. Drops of blood trickled down my arm. Picking up a few bananas left behind, I peeled them and coated their insides with saliva. A ketaki tree with a cluster of gnarled branches and uneven bark offered a quick ascent to me. It was easy to aim from there. Bali didn't notice the banana skins spread across his path. The swaggering monster slipped and fell face down, his lip split at the corner. Served him right. I walked away, leaving Bali laughing while nursing the pain. 'Tara!' he called out. 'You will pay for this.'

'Keep your warnings to yourself, ginger-faced monkey.' I mumbled with a skinless banana in my mouth.

Ravan stayed for a few days. He engaged in wrestling matches with Bali. Sugreev didn't like this friendship. He kept his distance, without any explanation. As much as Bali was courteous, Sugreev waited for the riddance of this guest. Sugreev's behaviour wasn't strange to me. He was possessive about Bali – never appreciating anyone becoming too dear to him. Bali and Ravan's friendship was one of titans – they'd play games and discuss economics. Often, one would outsmart the other and share leadership advice. They spent long hours together, with Bali telling his new friend about his vision for the monkey-land and Ravan recounting underworld cases from the Asur history. Had I not seen them with my own eyes, I, too, would never have believed that such a mighty Rakshas could reveal his woes so sincerely to an animal.

Sugreev was suddenly alone, attention-starved and unsure of what his life meant.

During one such wrestling match, as everyone cheered wildly, I found him perched on top of a tree, staring at the sky.

'Hey, how many?' I shouted from below.

He glanced down briefly. 'What "how many"?'

'The stars. Counting them, eh?' I chuckled.

'Go and do what you do best – hover around the big monkey and seduce him. What are you even doing here?' he shot back, clearly irritated.

Red-faced, I started climbing the tree to break a bamboo pole on his head. But once I was closer, he suddenly said, 'Tara, keep Bali away from Ravan. He is ...,' Sugreev hesitated, 'a nuisance. A negative influence. Evil.'

'Why would you say that? You sent him to Bali in the first place,' I questioned. The bamboo fell from my hands.

'I thought Bali would toss him on the other side of the mountain. I never expected him to bring home a friend,' he bitterly spat the remnants of whatever he was chewing. 'Can't you see, Tara?

Are you blind? Ravan is in search of immortality; he is challenging the gods. How can he be good company for anyone? Explain this to the biggie, and he'd philosophize as "animals don't judge". Fine, we don't, but are we barred from thinking?'

My thinker friend was not a risk-taker like his twin. Bali believed in swift action. Sugreev was an observer – serious and poetic. He was different from the rest of the monkeys. Some even mocked him behind his back. What stung him the most was Bali's indifference to his concerns. Today was another such occasion. I settled beside him on a parallel branch.

'Shaitaan always leaves a little part of himself with everyone he meets. He can cloud your mind and obscure your intelligence if you are not well shielded,' Sugreev whispered. 'I'm feeling awkward. Very awkward. Evil attracts unconscious brains. Every bad experience of the affected then culminates into a series of bad decisions. Such is the power of Shaitaan. Get this pain off our backs, Tara. As soon as you can.'

'How?' I blurted unmindfully.

'Seduce him. Make him long for you and dump Ravan. Bear his child. Now's the right time.' Sugreev sat up excited.

'Shut up!' I erupted. 'I'd sooner drown in the Pampa than mother the child of your loony brother.'

Sugreev didn't tell me outright that I would walk into the bottom of the ocean should Bali hold my hand and lead me there. Why was he so restless? Animal instincts seldom go wrong. I kept fidgeting over it. Ravan was well behaved; compared to when he had first barged into Kishkindha, he had shown an unexpected transformation. I pondered and let it go, but the concern returned again and again. Vayu's curse – Indra's son ...

The very next day Ravan left our land. Both Sugreev and I breathed a sigh of relief.

14

'Bali, do you still love me?' I asked aloud, sitting amid the banana beds.

'Loving you hurts, Tara. I wish I had left my love on the earth,' his voice whispered through the plantations.

'Our marriage was a political alliance for you,' I reminded.

'Only partially,' his confession pierced through my heart.

'Why didn't you tell me before?' I felt helpless, hopeless.

'Why do you think I settled down? You really believe that I could be lured by the kingship of an unfamiliar realm? You were sensitive, and I was desperate.' Bali took a long pause. I could hear his rapid breathing,

the way he did when we made love. 'Desperation is shameful on earth. After death, nothing matters. There is no shame in owning the truth.'

'At least you don't have these groves and orchards, where your footsteps are yet to fade from the soil. Your laughter and my banter still echo on the plains,' I said sadly. 'How could you not think of me before falling to death?' I accused, sobbing.

'It was my destiny, Tara, earned by my father when his vajra had struck little Hanuman,' Bali tried to console. He offered only words, devoid of touch. My skin blazed with longing.

Was I to blame his father now for my loss? What use was it anyway? Bali wouldn't return.

'It is very lonely here,' I lamented. 'Son Angad will find his partner in due time. Ruma and Sugreev are together. I feel inadequate.' Bali remained quiet, unable to resolve my despair.

Wasn't he as lonely without me?

'It pains to look at Sugreev these days,' I continued. 'He looks exactly like you. I try to stay away. But this is a small place, and our paths keep crossing. Sometimes I wonder, what if he comes up someday and declares that

it was all a pathetic joke, that he is Bali and Sugreev is dead,' I gasped.

My heart ached. Bali went back to his silence. So numb was this overwhelming evening – the daylight, like a parasite, glided awkwardly towards dusk.

15

So beautiful was this reticent twilight – the daylight, like honey, receded gently towards dusk. Seated underneath a large tree, I wrote my first essay in my own script. We had made significant progress by now. Most of our basic sounds had a representative symbol. For those that didn't, we blended two or more symbols together to express the complex phonetics. We had begun transferring words onto tree barks and leaves, storing them in shadowy places safe from being blown away, drowned or burnt by nature. We, however, is an overstatement. Sugreev came and went. Sometimes he would follow Bali wherever he went. Or he would join Nal and Nil at Rishyamukh. He would return with a collection of poetry, orally composed, inspired by the beauty of sunset and the wavy, rocky landscapes. His poems featured the sages who lived there, Hanuman in meditation, Bali with his mace and the dense forest sprawled beside the tranquil Pampa. At times they hinted at his wife's medical recipes, from which he seemed distanced, while she admired his aloofness. I pretended not to hear the melancholic undertone. Ruma had made it clear to him that she had no fondness for rhyming words or metaphors; straight talk would please her more. The brooding poet eventually sought solace in his only friend, requesting help to preserve his compositions. That's when I started writing seriously.

This morning, I was writing about my pregnancy. I could feel myself growing plump by the day. I would experience sudden hunger pangs followed by long stretches when I had no desire to eat a single morsel. Ruma would cajole me to eat. My father was thrilled, checking on my well-being every now and then, with polite affection.

He dreamt of grooming a granddaughter into a great medical researcher. A successor to Ruma, unlike his own offspring. He instructed Ruma to spend more time with me, share details about her studies so that the baby could absorb knowledge even if the would-be mother wouldn't. Little did he know, the unborn child's father was expecting an empathetic leader. As for the would-be uncle, he yearned for a spiritual scholar, akin to Hanuman. Too many aspirations were mounting. Kishkindha was floating in an air of jubilance.

I was writing about these and more.

'Pregnant women get temperamental, I'd heard. But cryptic sketches on leaves are a first,' Bali's voice floated down. He hung from a branch above, his tail dangling over my head. I pulled it, making him fall with the broken branch gripped in his fingers. 'What are you doing?' He lifted my leaf to inspect it.

'We've created a script, Bali. Our script. Sugreev and I. I'm documenting my pregnancy days. When our child grows up, he will read it,' I said happily.

Sugreev joined us and stood beside a nearby tree, his arms crossed. Bali's face darkened. 'Still engrossed in a human ritual?'

My smile disappeared. Bali referred to humans when he wanted to abuse. I didn't mind being compared to humans, as long as it did not come from him.

'How does it matter?' Sugreev defended. 'If Tara is intelligent enough to acquire a skill monopolized by humans, it's good for us.'

'We don't need anything from the humans. Animals have their own distinct excellence,' Bali groaned. I was alarmed. If it was not for me, Bali would have been far more aggressive. Sometimes, Sugreev could be stubbornly dispassionate.

'Bali!' Sugreev called out sceptically. 'It's been very long. Let it go. Don't judge the entire race from our limited experience.' He continued trying to convince his brother, 'Humans are rational thinkers. We are at an advantage if we adopt their strengths.'

'True, they are good at thinking up deceitful tricks.' Bali was adamant. 'Treacherous. Cowards.'

He went on, 'I would trust a snake with its hood raised. But a human, never.'

Unknowingly, he had clutched the trunk of a guava tree, almost uprooting it. 'Stop,' I shouted. He promptly loosened his grip. This wasn't about me. Bali was once again battling with an unsettled past. Somewhat frightened, I rose to stand between them. 'Bali, if my writing troubles you, I will give it up. Tell me.'

'Yes, tell her,' Sugreev grunted. 'She has spent a lifetime putting this in order. It has been her only dream long before we both entered these forests. She spent years developing a script for the monkeys. Now, if the great king of Kishkindha commands her to drop it, she will gladly comply.'

Sugreev was visibly angry. I patted his hand, signalling him to calm down. Never had he spoken up for himself in front of his twin the way he fought for me.

Bali's eyes stilled on me before moving to Sugreev. 'Save the drama for another day,'

He softly instructed and shifted his attention back to me. 'Who am I to stop you, Tara?' he sighed. 'But remember, the first expressions that come through the body and voice are original. Everything contrived later has an element of artificiality. The impulse of your present is your only truth. Any afterthought is either a reflection of your past or an anticipation of the future.'

Bali was Bali. I opened my mouth to argue, as did Sugreev. He brought his hands up to touch my cheek and Sugreev's. Thud! He knocked our heads together.

'Ginger in your mouth.' I chattered, massaging my head.

'It's fine, Tara, not his fault.' Sugreev whispered, loud enough for Bali to hear. 'He has the body of a monkey and the brain of a frog. Not intellectual like you.' He shook his head left and right, trying to lighten the air.

'If you are finished flirting with others' wives, follow me. We have pending work to complete,' Bali said, and I kicked him. Sugreev kept his response vague. The brothers marched forward to attend to some great business that could not wait.

I heard Bali murmur, 'Keep her away from our past, you fool. Why bring that up with her?'

'Your turmoil, your past, your wife. It would be nice if you remembered.' Sugreev retorted disdainfully. Bali slapped his back hard, causing him to groan in pain.

I thought I didn't care any longer, but my eyes watered anyway.

The two had not gone too far when loud commotion perplexed us. A young voice, followed by a daunting male voice. Birds resting on the branches flew off in haste – something was happening on the banks of the Pampa. Within moments, more women shouted at the top of their lungs. The monkeys were in danger. Bali ran first, followed by Sugreev. I was just about to spring onto the nearest tree and leap across the branches when Bali suddenly turned, raised a finger reminding me not to, before disappearing into the woods. I stopped and walked slowly towards the lake.

Right when life had fallen into a peaceful rhythm, Dunduvi was back to reset the calm.

*

Girls from the tribe had been frolicking in the mud and sand, tossing each other into the waters of the Pampa, their whoops and laughs filling the air. Unbeknownst to them, a monster had been hiding someplace nearby. Assured that Bali wasn't present, he had charged at them. A wave of shock swept through the girls.

By the time we reached, Dunduvi was advancing towards Lali, the youngest of them all. She retreated slowly. He laughed at her like a maniac, making vulgar insinuations about her developing breasts and long legs, coaxing her to accompany him to the soft beds of cotton with gold-lined strands that she had never imagined existed. Lali's back was about to hit the banyan tree in the corner. Its tangled prop shoots twirled downwards into thickly matted braids, casting haunting shadows on the base to darken it like night. The other monkeys surrounding them were sweating by now and wanted to shriek but their voices were lost. Dunduvi stretched his hand out, cornering Lali further into the enclosure she was wilfully entering. Just before the threat got hold of her, she swung upwards, holding a prop shoot and reached the top of the tree, startling Dunduvi and everyone else. She jumped from above, holding a large mace and crying hoarsely. A massive blow landed on Dunduvi's back, breaking his spine. The monster howled in pain. Before everyone from the forest arrived, he raced out.

Lali was still standing there with the mace – shivering, raging, weeping, abusing. Others surrounded her, unsure of how to approach the girl. I moved forward and pulled her into a tight embrace. One by one, all the girls joined in. Ruma eventually freed her from the crowd, led her to the Pampa and threw her into the lake. She gulped, choked and recovered from the shock, pushing the water with her arms to swim back to us. My heart swelled with pride. From a distance, Bali and I exchanged a smile.

For days, I had taught the youth of Kishkindha how to use a mace. Sugreev trained them in wrestling. Bali joined us both, whenever he could. At strategic corners throughout the forest we planted our weapons, including the banyan by the Pampa. When everyone had lost their confidence in the face of danger, little Lali remembered her defence strategy.

That evening, Sugreev was very disturbed. The sugarcanes Ruma had chopped for him were left untouched. She called for me.

'It is fine, Sugreev. Go to sleep,' I advised.

'The pests. They never stop taking chances,' said Sugreev restlessly. 'He will come back again.'

There was no doubt that Dunduvi would not stop here. Kishkindha was on high alert. Bali was aware too.

'Everyone is prepared for him, or dangers greater than him. Calm down,' I tried to reassure.

'I know they are. That's not enough.' Sugreev sounded anxious. 'Many vicious forces come to

Bali – they leave as a friend or decide to stay away from him forever. They love him or they fear him.' He sat up, covering his face with his hands.

'So?' I sat on a lower branch of the tree; he came to join me.

'Tara, today we have made an enemy.'

I wondered what was bothering him about this development, especially when we had Bali.

'An enemy always returns with a propaganda. They want revenge. They strike repeatedly till they inflict irreversible damage.' Sugreev was abnormally stressed.

'What do you propose Lali should have done?' Ruma was thoroughly irritated. 'Fold her hands and request him to back off?'

Sugreev looked at her from the adjoining branch. 'Oh Ruma, no! Lali did the unthinkable. I am very proud of her. I am just trying to remain extra careful of the upcoming signals.' He hopped to the other branch to sit next to her. 'Next time, Dunduvi will target not one in the tribe, but he'd attempt to destroy our unity.'

Ruma pushed him with his elbow. 'Lali has

broken his back. Unlikely that he would stand straight again.'

'That's why I am worried,' said Sugreev. 'We have tormented him enough to motivate a recurrence, intending retaliation. Equal, if not larger.' He wiped his face with nervous fingers. 'Bali's backbone is in danger. We are not thinking about it.'

'Keep thinking, then.' Ruma turned to her side and jumped off, walking away from Sugreev's absurd concerns.

The younger monkey was not yet done. How different could the twins be! Bali dealt with problems head on. Sugreev's pessimism was such a stark contrast. I, too, got up to leave. Sugreev held me by the elbow. 'Tara, I need your help. Bali won't listen to me. He'll ridicule my fears. Ruma has blind faith in him. You support me in strengthening Bali. This is not about the spine inside his body. Our love is his backbone.'

I nodded, promising I would. Sugreev had been there for my script. If there was anything I could do for him, may it be this.

That night, I couldn't sleep. The leaves fluttering, birds calling, even a grasshopper darting ahead – a variety of mundane sounds jolted me awake every time my eyes closed. Bali slept soundly beside me, one of his hands caressing my belly. I hugged him. Sugreev's fears kept playing inside my brain. 'There is nothing called one enemy,' he said before letting me go. 'Enemy's friends also become our enemies. We will need our own friends. Responsible ones. The jungle won't be safe any longer if we continue to live in isolation.'

The next day started earlier than usual. Bali was off to pray. Lali had recovered sufficiently. Once referred to as the silly little darling, she had turned into an icon for the tribe overnight. While she simultaneously enjoyed and detested the newfound attention, Sugreev seemed to have gone mad. He came somersaulting towards me even before he had eaten a morsel. Ruma waited for him, holding a bunch of bananas. Usually, this was when he would gobble down his food with a world of appetite. When he showed no interest, she dumped them on the ground, sat with her legs open and prepared to devour them by herself. I didn't know whether to laugh or cry.

'Tara, call all the birds in the forest. Right now.' I did as he wanted. The winged creatures gathered in no time. Even the owls and the cuckoos responded. 'Tell them,' he instructed. 'They must fly out as far and wide as possible, informing every monkey and bear they meet, in whatever way they can, of a grand forest kingdom called Kishkindha. This is a dense forest next to a lake with crystal clear waters, blessed with the wealth of fruits and vegetables. Monkeys and bears have a dominion of their own here, ruled by the great Bali. Go!'

I could fairly gather what Sugreev was doing. He was trying to empower the tribe by inviting more of its likes. This had not been discussed with Bali. He would have dismissed any need for such maneuvering. He'd accuse Sugreev of being lame. The younger twin was counting on me to persuade his brother. It was easier that way. Less mockery, no refusal. I looked at Ruma. She was busy munching on the bananas, a mountain of peels stacked beside her.

'Come on, what are you waiting for? Tell them,' Sugreev prodded. I translated for the gathering and handed over thin leaves with 'Kishkindha' written on each of them. Most of the birds flew away immediately. Only the nasty owls sat erect, unwilling to move, with no questions asked – their notorious eyes pointing at me like a trap. I picked up a stone to throw at them. Sugreev snatched it from me. 'Just do as they say; let it be their day for once,' he pleaded.

'I apologize for all the mimicry,' I said in a stiff voice, not meaning a word. They hooted triumphantly and soared away.

Sugreev fixed his eyes on the sky, watching the feathers slowly disappear. 'One last request.' His eyes gleamed with excitement. 'Even the smallest of the insects should sharpen their stings to defend against any unexpected attack. Tell all reptiles and insects to boost their poison and find the easiest way to replenish their venom, unless they are inexhaustible. Please.'

I assured him that the task would be done. He smiled gratefully and turned around, only to find Ruma sitting amidst a pile of banana peels, supplies for the day spent. With burning hunger gnawing at his gut, the poor monkey was out of words. Ruma burped aloud.

Without the birds, the land felt desolate. I missed their chirps. When the sky once again filled with the shrill familiar music of my feathered friends, I rushed to the edge of the Pampa. They were coming back in hordes. Sugreev came rolling to stand beside me, followed by Bali.

'What's happening? This looks like a festive reunion,' Bali remarked happily. 'What are they saying?'

'They are announcing that their mission has been accomplished,' I replied, thoroughly enjoying the tweets around, and my heart fluttering. Will my script be legible? Will they come?

'What mission?' Bali frowned.

I winked. 'Secret!'

Before long, they started to arrive. I was elated. My script was working. The animals did not need an interpreter! Sacred intelligence brewed amid the wild. Profound joy rendered me speechless. A large troupe of monkeys flocked in first, then a sloth of bears – both brown and black. Even a few deer joined. Last came an orphaned bull, its horns majestically curved, pleading for a home with tears streaming from its beautiful black eyes. Everyone had gathered at the fringes of the forest, seeking citizenship in Kishkindha.

'What is this!' Bali enquired, surprised. I shrugged. He looked at Sugreev. He, too, shook his head. None of us knew.

'Ruma?' Bali turned towards his favourite devotee. She was about to open her mouth when her husband intervened.

'You are still here? Jambavan is sitting with a hand on his stomach, complaining of diarrhoea. How forgetful of you.' He whisked her away to tend to the imaginary ailment of the great bear.

Bali was deep in thought for a while before he spoke again. 'This forest, our great abode of Kishkindha, has always opened its arms to the wandering nomads, offering a pleasant habitat to the migrants. Everyone is welcome here.'

Cheers erupted from the crowd. The vast forest unlatched its womb, providing shelter to the new entrants. Friendships blossomed. Watching a young fawn splashing in the waters of the Pampa alongside Lali warmed our hearts. Sugreev named the deer 'Angad', meaning an ornament. When Lali sat on his back, Angad bent his neck trying to prick her with his well-shaped antlers running in branches. Amid squeals of laughter, Lali dodged, saving herself from the naughty deer. Often, while I sat writing my essay, I would see the bull coiled between its feet, enjoying the breeze under a tree, dozing away.

As excitement soared, guilt raised its head. Had we done the right thing by keeping Bali in the dark?

16

The hardened dry creepers on the ground scratched at my back. I started to pull them out.

'Don't!' Bali's voice suddenly loomed. 'Don't clean. Nature is beautiful. Live with them. Adapt. Rearrange if you must, but do not remove.'

Bali had said this a long time ago when he was alive. His words echoed in my brain, causing my hands to slow down. More creepers entwined around my tail.

'Bali, are you around?' I called out.

'No,' pat came the sarcasm.

'How is Sita?' I asked. I had been thinking of her lately, as the beautiful, bejewelled queen of Ayodhya.

'She is not in Ayodhya.' He had read my mind.

'Why?' I was surprised.

'One person in Ayodhya cheated on his spouse. He later demanded his matrimonial rights back, just as the queen had received from the king. A few immoral supporters raised a debate over rights and rules. Swift action was imperative to curb the rapid spread of misinformation. Sita has been exiled,' Bali explained discreetly. My heart felt defunct.

'Exile! Meaning indefinite expulsion?' I was appalled. The picture I expected was of a happy family with children and elders in a glorious kingdom. 'Ram accepted the separation?'

'No one can separate Ram and Sita. They are committed souls, together forever,' Bali pacified. 'The garbage inside human minds does not cleanse itself overnight. Sita was pregnant then. The couple preferred peace over luxury, securing her and the unborn child, instead of negotiating with opportunists.'

'That makes no difference. Sita is suffering,' I slammed his logic.

'A queen is exiled, Tara. The husband did not exile his wife. Sita's golden idol sits in Ram's private

chambers,' Bali reasoned. 'Ram is suffering equally, in the absence of his beloved.'

'Ram could have abandoned Ayodhya and accompanied Sita to the forest. A love story would have prevailed. Sita was worthy of his noble devotion, not the crooks.' I murmured. If I had to choose between Bali and Kishkindha, I wouldn't think twice.

The one I could let go of everything for, defended the one who had given up on his love. 'He cannot abandon Ayodhya unless he is defeated in battle or the people impeach him. Ram is a king first, husband later.'

Raj dharma! Nothing was personal; everything and everyone belonged to the kingdom. Even the time and emotions of the royalty were accountable. The country was the priority; personal relationships came later. The pledge of leadership. I closed my eyes.

'Is this the Ayodhya Sita dreamt of?' I mourned, remembering the wonderful woman I had met only once. I couldn't return to Bali; Sita wouldn't return to Ram. How strange were the verdicts of destiny!

'Sita's dreams led to a prosperous Ayodhya, empowering the people with wisdom, wealth and efficiency,' Bali said. 'A bunch of empowered people

turned into sly activists – moulding information and misusing liberties, exploiting causes to raise noise. Activists are always scared of changemakers.'

'Ravan sinned by pulling apart Ram and Sita. Now the great sin is repeated by the nice people of Ayodhya.' I remarked sadly. 'Would there be a war again?'

'Yes, there will be another war, of a different kind,' Bali philosophized. 'In the living world, minds can be inspired by both Bhagwan and Shaitaan. Those who opt for the path of darkness, still expect light and love from the divine, resulting self-conflicts.'

I shook my head in remorse. Politics is such a deceptive symphony of inspiring promises that end up destroying everything beautiful! Either by death, like me and Bali, or by separation, like Sita and Ram.

'One lens is inadequate to view life, Tara. Don't feel miserable,' my husband consoled me. I kept quiet. 'Few people at Ayodhya wanted to exploit sinful possibilities by misinterpreting facts. That ploy has been thwarted. Had Sita not gone, gossip and misdeed would have flourished behind closed doors. Now, they are compelled to confront the consequences, enforcing law and order among the masses. Why don't you understand?'

Here was a dead king talking and a living woman responding. In pursuit of social justice, one woman's disrespect was no more than a minor sacrifice. I fumed, I sighed.

'Where is Sita now?'

'Far away in the forest, where the three rivers meet, at the hermitage of Rishi Valmiki. She is a mother now. And guess what? She has given birth to twins. Much like Sugreev and me.'

I ignored the last part. What was so great about twins? I didn't want to think about the monkey brothers. 'Can't we bring Sita here? I think I should talk to Hanuman.'

'Don't,' he advised. 'Hanuman knows everything. He is connected with Ram in more ways than one. Sita is safe.'

Humans. They create civilizations and societies in pursuit of prosperity, yet often end up inflicting misery upon each other to assert superiority. We, on the contrary, are merely denizens of the jungle – uncivilized beings who attack when cornered.

'You were always wise, Bali,' I said disdainfully. 'Trust a seven-hooded snake if you have to, but never a human.'

17

The evening before, there was untimely rain. The ground was damp, the weather cosy. Lali slept peacefully with her arm girdling Angad, the beautiful fawn safe in her company. Early rays of the sun filtered through chunks of clouds, between brief drizzles.

If the romance between the sun and the rain was not enough, endearing warmth burgeoned between the twins with a rare display of affection. After returning from his morning prayers, Bali draped an arm around Sugreev's shoulders. 'Remember how you used to sleep as a child?' he asked, nodding towards Angad and Lali.

'No, I don't.' Sugreev smiled. 'I only remember how you tied me to the highest branch of a banyan tree with your tail when the forest felt scary.' Bali smiled, gently ruffling Sugreev's fur. 'The squabbling birds with pointed beaks came flying, claiming their reserved spots. You warned them of dire consequences should I be touched,' the younger twin added. Sweet memories!

'Oh, how they squawked! I understood nothing, but their defiant chirping left little to the imagination,' the twins laughed hysterically, the protruding teeth covering more than half their faces.

When Bali learnt that he was going to be a father, he wasn't overwhelmed. 'As if the female wasn't enough already, she is launching another weapon now,' he remarked.

Before I could throw a stone, Anjani ma scolded him, shocking us. 'Say something auspicious, you ginger-mouth! Wait for the little one to jump higher than your arrogance.' She had always been very fond of the elder twin. The transition from a motherly figure to a grandmother had inspired a sharp switch in loyalty.

Sugreev danced around with glee; Ruma made no attempts to stop him. She had prepared a list of places I should not venture into within the forest and fruits I should not eat. Father visited from time to time, checking my nerves or just observing from a distance and declaring, 'She's fine. The baby is growing well.'

'Another wanderer is on his way out, ready to work his charm on Mother Earth.' Bali whispered as he sat in the banana groove, his hand caressing my belly. 'Soon, Bali will be known as the father of Tara's child.' I turned to him, hugging and kissing his smiling lips, tears glistening in my eyes.

This was Bali's excitement in a nutshell. Even the owls showed affection with enhanced tolerance towards my hoots, mimicking their nocturnal conversations. Sugreev would annoy Ruma, repeatedly asking when he would get to see the baby. Bali patiently waited for nature to take its course. His fatherly instincts surfaced in undeclared moments, like this morning, when he reminisced about nurturing his brother.

Lali remained deep in sleep. Angad opened his eyes. Without moving his head, he mapped the tree from which restored rainwater dripped. From the corner of his eyes, he glanced at us and finally at Lali – her hands wrapped around his neck. Suddenly, he got up with a jerk and ran as fast as he could. Lali hung from his neck like a garland. It didn't take her too long to lose the grip and fall, waking up in utter confusion, while we laughed uncontrollably behind her. She quickly gathered what had happened and chased after Angad, calling him a shameless rat.

*

Labour started late in the day. Bali was training the tribe on flexible metabolism. They were immersed in activities designed to speed up or slow down chemical reactions in their bodies, adapting to various climates and seasonal harvests. The monkeys were learning to control and preserve energy, while simultaneously boosting their aerobic capacities. I joined in on the exhilarated cheers, sitting a few yards away. A jostling twinge in my belly was followed by cramps in the beginning before a sudden pain shot up.

'Ruma!' I cried out. My voice probably didn't even reach the nearest herbs. Panting, I looked up when Bali jumped in from nowhere. He lifted me in his arms and ran back to the tribe – calling out for Ruma, my father and Anjani ma. Eyes closed in deep pain, breathing unevenly, I clutched onto Ruma. Anjani ma ridiculed Bali. 'All this while he feigned indifference, as if the birth of his child was no big deal. When the moment came, he gathered the entire tribe as if a monkey is giving birth for the first time. I had recognized his pretence right at the beginning.'

The pain kept rising and falling sporadically. Every time I tried to sit up, thinking it to be a false alert, the cramps returned. I shrieked and fell backwards. The trees sent breeze from all directions, birds cheered from above. A large section of the tribe stood in a circle, maintaining safe distance. The children were instructed to leave the premises and play elsewhere. I panted again and stretched my head, trying to see Bali. He was rolling from one spot to the other like a fallen guava.

The pain struck again. I felt like a thousand needles were pricking me from the inside. I pushed and pulled back. And tried again. I changed my posture to sit upright, pelvis outstretched and knees pressed to my chest. The baby was on its way out. With a steady hand, I gently reached for the infant facing downwards, and severed the umbilical cord with the other. The baby buried its head in my chest. A soft, furry creature. A boy. Slumping back from the colossal strain, I lay flat on the ground. The baby latched onto my breast and began feeding itself, as I lactated heavily. 'Energetic and confident.' Father smiled happily from a distance. 'Learns before being prompted.' I closed my eyes, trying to relax. The little thing on my chest wriggled gently. I caressed his back, assuring that he had reached his destination safely.

Some yards away, Bali had raised a ruckus. 'He is my child; I want to hold him,' he demanded.

Anjani ma blocked his path. 'Great king of Kishkindha, you must not go beyond this mark.' She chuckled. 'Fathers are not supposed to go near the newborn. No one is allowed. He will be brought to you as per the protocol in a few days.'

'Days! Protocol!' The poor monkey was at a loss for words.

'It's a medical precaution, Bali.' Ruma's voice made him turn. 'You may have noticed that none of us have gone too close to Tara all this while. Please understand.'

Severely upset, he sat down and gazed at me. The child had fallen asleep now. I gestured that everything was fine.

If only everything were really fine!

The tribe was filled with joy as they welcomed a new member. Suddenly, the tranquil vibes were replaced by a cacophony of despair, unlike anything I had ever heard in the past. The earth trembled. Terror gripped the faces of all present. Those were the voices of Kishkindha's children – shrieks of anguish, distress, fear. Of chaos and stampede. Everyone scattered swiftly, unsure of what had caused the commotion. Bali sprang up and vanished, followed by Sugreev.

Left sitting alone, my heart pounded loudly. My newborn protested with a mild quiver. The sound of my throbbing heart was too startling for him. Something must have gone terribly wrong. A different kind of roar echoed from the horizon. Not the familiar voices of monkeys or bears. This was something else. I prayed for the safety of our tribe.

From afar, mournful laments enveloped the air of Kishkindha. I started sobbing without knowing what had happened, as my hands kept comforting the baby. After what felt like an eternity, I heard footsteps approaching. Tired, lost, devastated, angry, tearful. From different mouths, fragmented information floated in.

The children were playing in the blackberry orchards, while the harmless bull watched from a distance. As the elders got busy with me, its demeanour changed. It rose with a jerk, its body swelled with aggression, and it charged ferociously towards the unsuspecting group. No one was ready for this. Before they could register the attack, some of the young ones were trampled under the bull's hooves – smashed to death. Panic ensued as the others wailed and scuttled helter-skelter.

The mad bull ploughed through the vegetable patch, goring the children on the way with its fierce horns, relentlessly chasing Lali. She ran recklessly, but alas! The bull anticipated her every move, blocking her path and entrapping her, thereby forcing her to drift away from all the places where the weapons had been hidden. With a deafening roar, the bull lunged at Lali, intent on crushing her to the ground.

Just then, Angad sprang forward to thrust himself between Lali and the bull. His shapely antlers broke into pieces with the enormous collision. The beautiful fawn convulsed, collapsing onto the earth. The knock ruptured the belly of the writhing bull, exposing the violent Dunduvi hiding inside. With a final lunge Dunduvi put an end to Angad, before fleeing in haste, sparing a chilling look at Lali and promising to come back for her later.

Bali and Sugreev's whereabouts were unknown. Time froze. Lali sat motionless across Angad. All my happiness from a few hours before had lost its sheen. It was a dark day for the residents of Kishkindha. Mangled bodies of the children lay before their parents. The forest was swept over with shock and disbelief.

Unaware of the turmoil unfolding around us, the baby latched onto me again for its due share of milk. Quietly, I got up and stepped out of confinement. This was not the hour for rest or restraint. The sky was overcast. The air dusty. From somewhere, Bali's voice thundered. 'Traitors have no place in this world. You hear, everyone? Everyone?'

God knows who he was addressing. With horrified eyes unable to comprehend what was to follow, I clasped the baby to my breast. Another thundering howl rose from the earth. 'Every traitor will have to die the most gruesome death.' The animals rushed ahead, coming out of their temporary hideout. Bali stood at the edge of Kishkindha. He had lifted Dunduvi above his head with both hands, his mouth unleashing a barrage of ghastly profanities. Dunduvi lay dead between his hands, his head smashed by the mace, fragments of bones falling off.

'Died too soon, monster! Bali isn't done yet. Come back with more traitors whom I can kill. Go, get them.' With another primal roar that jolted the earth and the sky, he hurled the corpse with enormous force. The huge lifeless body with hanging flesh soared towards Rishyamukh, leaving a trail of blood, flesh and torn ligaments on its way.

Bali fell to the ground and wept.

Sugreev held him from behind, trying to offer solace and lift him up, reminding him of his newborn and wife. Bali heard nothing. He pushed Sugreev aside and limped towards the blackberry orchard. The tribe followed, I trailed behind them. The place looked like a crematorium. Bali forged ahead amid hiccups, shedding tears at every step where a child lay dead.

He stopped abruptly when Lali stood up. Slowly, she approached him, her voice coarse. 'Didn't you say that as long as there is Bali, everyone in the forest is safe?' The tribe stood stunned at the little monkey's audacity. She leapt forward and struck him on the chest. 'Answer me, King. How could Angad die? Why are there so many unrecognizable, dead faces here? Where were you when Dunduvi attacked me, for the second time?'

Bali knelt before her. 'Forgive me, little one.'

Sugreev and Ruma tried to intervene, but Bali stretched his tail to barricade the space between him and Lali. All could see but none were to interfere.

'God will punish you. The deaths of the innocent will haunt you for as long as you live. You will not be forgiven by their poor souls.' After pronouncing her curse, Lali disappeared from sight. Bali stayed kneeling with his head held low.

The day was not over yet.

*

One by one everyone left, to allow Bali the respite he so badly needed and to gather themselves after the long, tragic hours. Angad's body lay a few yards away. Bali stared at him, his gaze unwavering. I wanted to go near him, with the baby in my arms. Sugreev vehemently shook his head. 'Don't even try. Not now.'

I sat down, watching my husband. Only a few steps could take me to him. Yet, this distance seemed endless. Something invisible separated all of us from him. The shame of a proud king.

The night was ominous. An unsettling riddle was reshaping the truth of the terrain. The deaths of children. The first rebel in Kishkindha. A beloved king suddenly left alone. Eyes full of life staring at the dead ones. It seemed to ensnare us in a disturbing spell, hovering around like a fierce insect with venomous stings. When the haze would strangle us, no one knew. Yet I couldn't pull Bali out of its way. Access was denied. Gently, I tapped the sleeping child on my shoulder. He woke up with a shrill cry. His father still didn't turn around. As if he had begun his journey to another world. As if Angad was sucking Bali's life force into his lifeless eyes.

How could Sugreev not feel what I did?

The sounds of footsteps on the tall grass hurt our ears amid the suffocating silence. Hanuman walked in with a grim expression. Sugreev leapt ahead to catch up with him. They looked at me and Bali, discussing something serious. I got up. They stopped when I drew closer.

'Pishachini Tara is a mother now, dear brother,' I said, showing the child. Hanuman gently touched the child's head with the back of his hand and smiled with deep affection. I glanced at him gratefully for the blessings. 'What more has gone wrong, Brother? Why are you here?'

Sugreev attempted to dismiss any such possibility. But Hanuman and I had known each other since the day I was born.

'Bad news, Tara,' Hanuman breathed heavily. 'Rishi Matanga was praying at his hermitage on Rishyamukh Mountain this evening. That is when the blood, bones and muscles of Dunduvi's body came hurtling towards him. Chopped parts fell on the clean ground, prepared for a fire sacrifice.' Hanuman stopped to clear his throat. I closed my eyes, expecting the worst. 'Enraged, the sage pronounced a curse. *Whoever has done this will die instantly should those unholy feet ever step upon the pure rocks of Rishyamukh.*'

Hanuman paused. I waited for a while and looked up. 'Is that all? Nothing more?'

Hanuman looked surprised, Sugreev thought I had gone mad.

'Sorry, Brother,' I apologized, patting the restless little creature on my lap back to sleep. 'At this juncture, I should just simplify problems.' I smiled wearily. 'The solution is staring us in the face. Bali can't go to Rishyamukh.' I nodded in acceptance. 'So, he will not go. I will go, or Sugreev will, if there's anything urgent.'

Hanuman raised his hand to touch my head, uttering a prayer. When he finished, I added, 'If Rishyamukh is ever in trouble, tell the sage that Bali will not be available for any service.'

We laughed together, trying our best to escape

the heavy burdens weighing upon us. Sugreev appeared quite relieved by my decisive threat countering the curse of the sage. Fool! He had forgotten that Hanuman lived there.

18

'Bali, it was my stupidity. I am to be blamed for everything.'

I walked, rudderless, through the blackberry orchard, stopping at the spot where Angad had breathed his last. In so many years nothing had changed. Even the memories were raw. Seemed just a few days ago.

'No, Tara,' Bali asserted. 'Sugreev tried to help. You supported him. Your intentions were noble.'

'The results were devastating.' I pondered in repentance for collaborating with Sugreev and hiding facts from Bali. With Angad's death, the once-beautiful Lali had become bitter. Bali himself had grown irritable and short-tempered. The cute, reclusive Jambavan was

more alert and reactive, no longer drunk on dreams of honey. Everyone was in a state of agitation. The trust of the forest towards its residents declined. Guests were no longer welcomed. Passersby hurried through the woods quickly, without stopping for rest, as the eerie hospitality of the inhabitants felt more scary than pleasant. Even the internal citizenship was divided. The original population were distinguished as loyalists, othering the outsiders who joined later. They brought the traitor – the loyalists accused.

'It was never about you,' Bali interjected, shutting down my self-blame. 'It was about me. I thought all along that Bali alone is enough to protect the forest-dwellers. It was an arrogant assumption, not a progressive decision. I had sufficient power, but one brain cannot brainstorm.'

'I feel terrible, Bali,' I cried. 'We shouldn't have opened our doors to immigrants, making way for Dunduvi to infiltrate.'

'Tara, we never had doors, remember?' Bali's gentle voice was steeped in tender affection.

It was true; he believed the wild was his kingdom, and he belonged to the wild. Vast and endless. Doors were for parochial civilizations. 'The new settlers had brought the saviour deer. Otherwise Dunduvi was an old enemy. He would have ambushed, one way or the other.'

My voice choked. 'I wonder at times why you had named our son "Angad".'

He sighed. 'So that I never forget his unfortunate namesake. A father and a king hoped to recreate a story in which someone called Angad is invincible.'

'You know why I didn't object?' I sighed in return. 'I thought the world would always need one Angad who wouldn't shy away from offering himself as a wall, when there is danger on one side and fragile lives on the other.'

19

Angad ran like a young, energetic fawn, dodging the gigantic trees and jumping over the thick mesh of bushes. I threw banana peels in his way, but he skipped over them as if he had eyes on the soles of his feet. The sal and the tamal trees laughed at my plight.

'Stop, or else you will get slapped on your back,' I warned. My threat fell on deaf ears. Ruma ran from another direction, offering bribes of ripe guavas and fat bananas to entice him. Jambavan panted, with promises of having collected the best stories where monkeys outwitted tigers. Nothing worked. The young lad refused to fall into the traps laid by elders, his mind conspiring adventures that the adults wouldn't approve of.

Just the other day, he disappeared from the forest, only to be escorted back by Hanuman. Meanwhile, Sugreev was wrestling with Jambavan. The great bear had taken a liking to this new activity of late. His loose skin started tightening, his protruding belly receded. After receiving a few blows on his arms and shoulder, he grew irate at the impudence of his opponent.

The arrival of Hanuman made them stop. Sugreev touched the feet of Hanuman to pay his respects. The great bear lifted his hand to plant one punch. Before he could strike, Bali jumped in between from nowhere, offending Jambavan immensely.

'Play fair, Jambavan. Treachery is the mark of the weak.' His advice left his audience fuming. There was a strange anger on Bali's face. I knew where it came from, Jambavan didn't.

A confrontation seemed imminent had Hanuman not intervened. 'Bali is right,' he said calmly, disappointing those awaiting a gossip-worthy clash. 'Treachery begets inconclusive tales shrouded with uncertainty.'

Bali scanned Hanuman's serene face. 'What do you mean?'

'Nothing. This one.' Hanuman pointed at Angad. All attention shifted to the young monkey, his eyes hazel like his father's. Hanuman glanced at Sugreev and me. 'Climbed up Rishyamukh this morning. In one go. Without stopping, he ran right to the top. Such an attempt deserves applause from the king.' He smiled.

Bali turned towards Angad. The child looked down, unsure whether he would be praised or rebuked.

'You climbed Rishyamukh in one go?' Bali asked. Angad nodded. 'But you still can't swim up and down the Pampa in one breath,' he was reminded.

'I will do that too, faster than you,' Angad promised with a frown. Everyone laughed.

'Every time you promise and disappoint yourself,' Bali said, walking away.

'Next time I won't.' Angad followed him, thumping the ground thrice with his leg.

I shook my head in frustration. This was going to be yet another day when I would have to pull the father and son out of the lake in the middle of the day, after they had competed enough. Bali would never let him win. Angad would never be convinced that he would lose again if they tried one more time. When the two were far away, I stepped towards Hanuman. 'What was he doing at Rishyamukh?'

Hanuman took a long, deep breath. 'He pulled the roofs off the huts at Rishi Matanga's hermitage, broke some bamboo pillars that held the roofs in place, all the while shouting – "bring the sage that cursed my father. I want to see who stopped the mighty Bali from entering Rishyamukh. Fight with the prince, come."' Hanuman covered his face with his hands, laughing. The coconut trees gasped. I was about to faint but wanted to thrash Angad first. Sugreev stood there shaking in terror, wondering what new curse must have befallen us with this development. Ruma praised the guts of the little monkey that no one else showed in the tribe. 'Seems Angad is following the inspiration of his Uncle Hanuman. Should I call Anjani ma or spill the legends of your childhood myself?'

Hanuman chuckled, joining Ruma in sharing the exuberance. 'Don't worry, Tara,' he said, carefully avoiding Ruma's reference to the legends. 'The sages are travelling for pilgrimage, the hermitage is empty. I will set everything in order.'

I remembered all these and more, as I chased my son to stop him from attempting another reckless stunt. But I was certain he'd return with an avalanche of complaints.

Last time he had polished off some of the medical concoctions prepared by Father. 'Don't try the potions left there. Not even if the bad doctor insists.' Eyes flung wide, he counselled the poor animals suffering from one ailment or the other, waiting to be healed. 'They are nauseating! Yuck!' He spat out whatever little remained on his tongue. The boy confessed later that he was inspecting the tastes.

'It's fine,' Ruma barged in, before Father could pick up his bamboo stick and break it on the thief's back. Standing between Angad and Father, she promised to personally deliver fresh medicines to the patients later. No wonder Ruma was the 'good doctor' for Angad; he called my father the 'bad doctor'.

Father scolded her for defending the spoilt child. 'Like mother, like son,' he grunted.

I wish my son were not like me. That he'd be like Bali. Or Sugreev. Or Father. Ruma. Jambavan. Anyone, for all I cared. Just not like me. It was becoming so difficult to manage him. I remembered how I embarrassed my father with my mischiefs, incessant questions and disobedience during my childhood. Angad was copying my behaviour now. I slapped my forehead, in repentance of the tough times I had once put my father through.

Angad had been unusually distracted of late. In the morning, I had caught him drawing some patterns on the sand on the banks of the Pampa. It looked like a map. The moment he saw me studying his diagrams, he hastily erased them and bolted. We had been running since. I was out of breath now.

'Aaaaahhhhhhhh!'

With a shriek, I slipped on a banana peel and fell. I sat down clutching my leg in pain. Ruma stopped and turned around, torn between attending to me and continuing with the chase. Jambavan kept calling out to him. I groaned, clasping my feet with a hand. 'Well deserved.' The owls and the cuckoos chimed in from above. Ginger in their mouth!

With my head buried between my knees, one hand soothing my ankle, I could hear footsteps amidst the rustle of leaves. I smelt him too. When I didn't look up, he jumped before me and started nursing my ankle with his little hands. I grabbed him, turned him upside down on my lap and smacked him on the buttocks. He flailed his arms and legs for mercy, promising never to trust me again. Once both of us had calmed down, I fed him bananas and guavas. The child was old enough to keep the world at his feet, but he preferred to be fed by his mother, especially after receiving a dose on his posterior.

'What were you up to?' I asked.

'I won't tell you.' he countered. It was time to negotiate secrets with my son.

'The diagram was wrong,' I said, startling him. 'The river in the north doesn't flow towards the west.' I ventured a guess.

'You know which way it flows? Tell me more,' he pleaded.

'What do you know and what is it that you don't know?' I had trapped him. He didn't suspect a thing.

'The earth is a mystery. Precious treasures are hidden within its bounteous folds,' he whispered a fantasy, looking at me with wide eyes. 'An invaluable treasure has gone missing from the shores of a magnificent river. Whether it lies below the soil or has sunk into the sea, no one knows. But the treasure still weeps, its torment haunts the air.'

I shivered. What stories had Bali been spinning for the child? I blinked back the vain tears flooding my eyes. Was talking to a child easier than sharing one's agony with the wife?

'So?' I asked with a straight face.

'So, I want to go and search for the treasure. And gift it to Father.' Innocence flashed brightly on his face.

'You love your father more than me?'

The answer was direct, obvious and unapologetic. 'Yes. You love Father more than me?' he asked back.

'Yes.' I returned the favour. But childhood was less complicated than adulthood.

'Why?' disappointment rang in his tone, his eyes overflowing.

'Why not?' I shrugged. He sat there miserably with his gaze fixed on the ground. I drew him closer and ran my fingers through his furry body. I didn't know how to say this, but I had to. 'Angad,' I tried. 'Don't ever go looking for your father's treasure.' He frowned. I searched for the right words. 'Each soul faces its own battles. The treasure is your father's battle, he should uncover it. Not us.'

My words seemed to get him thinking. I turned him towards me. The tiny hazel eyes resembling his father's blinked repeatedly. 'None of us are equipped for this. We don't know enough about the treasure or its secrets. Our intervention will only make it difficult for your father.'

'Why are you sad?' he interrupted, reaching out to touch my face.

'Not sad. Happy. You are a wonderful child.' I smiled.

'You are lying,' he insisted.

'You are blind,' I retorted.

*

'Angad needs defence skills. Scribbling symbols on leaves won't prepare him for life-battles.'

My hands slowed down. Angad turned.

'We've disagreed earlier too, Bali.' I replied. 'Why make it so sarcastic that fighting isn't fun any longer?'

Bali didn't argue. Angad, wise beyond his years, got up and followed his father without a word. Much of Angad's training was under Bali's supervision. From fighting to wrestling, and taking him along to the dense corners of the forest, to explaining the decisions of the elders and the unpredictability of nature and exposing him to various forms of life – be it the fish in the Pampa or eggs in the nests of the owls. The boy was growing up strong and steady.

I removed the leaf on which he was practising a script alongside me. He had made some quick diagrams before going after his father. A large monkey facing a lake. A small monkey walking away from him towards a tree in the corner of the leaf, where another monkey sat looking at the ground. He had promised to return once he was free from Bali.

Sometimes, Ruma and I watched them from afar. 'Show him the mysteries of the forest, Ruma,' I lamented. 'He hasn't explored that yet.'

She looked at me strangely. 'Relax, Tara. Who showed us all that when we were young?'

'No one distracted us to this extent either.'

Ruma patted my shoulder. 'Distractions were always there. Remember Hanuman's antics every other day?' We looked at each other and chuckled.

'The mystery of the forest pulsates on its own. It will embrace Angad too.' I heard her saying again. 'You chose your rhythm, I picked mine. Now let Angad discover his.'

*

Bali lifted him up with one hand and threw him to the ground. I jumped down from the tree. The child might have broken his shoulder. He was lying flat, motionless, with his face on the ground.

'Get up, idiot,' Bali commanded. 'Just one blow and this one falls to the ground. How will you tackle your enemies?' There was no response from Angad, no movement either. My eyes were bursting out by now, my feet shaking. 'Angad!' Bali roared again. No response. He quickly approached him and knelt by him. One hand moved forward to turn him. Before Bali could touch him, the boy leapt into the air, striking blows on his father's shoulder till the big monkey tumbled and fell on his back. The son spread his legs wide and landed right on his father's chest, rendering him motionless.

Taken aback, Bali laughed out loudly, patting his son on his arms. He made no attempts to get up. After a very long time, I saw him laughing. I turned to leave the two alone in their reverie. Ruma touched my shoulder and walked alongside.

I hadn't yet left the scene when Kishkindha shook again. Another calamity was on its way. Bali sprang up, as did Angad. Without wasting a moment, Ruma climbed up to the topmost branch of the tamal tree. From afar I could see Sugreev running towards us.

20

Every morning, the passing birds from faraway lands brought the news of growth and wreckage. And gossip. 'That river on the west is drying; expect animals to migrate – some might enter Kishkindha,' they discussed.

'Paw prints of a leopard have been traced on the soil,' was the discourse of another day. Jambavan attested to these reports. He had been following the grazing herd of deer every day, up and back, at Bali's request. The prints were unmissable on the moist mud.

'If you go straight and don't take a right or left, you will enter the menacing parts of the forest. You will hear wails of the departed, but none would be visible. Unhappy souls of dead animals loiter there, seeking a second chance to correct a few things that had gone wrong during their precious life.' This one stayed with me for long; I wrote about it in my daily notes. The spot they mentioned used to be a lover's corner sometime back, with romancing couples and mating pairs. Bali took me there sometimes, when he was only a lover and nothing else. It must have changed since the king of Kishkindha wore the crown of impatience and rudeness.

'The herd of deer had gone out to graze; they have returned like their backs are on fire,' Sugreev announced, panting hard. 'Things don't look fine to me. Tara, ask the birds.'

Bali shrugged. 'You feel something is wrong even when the clouds thunder and peacocks dance. What's new?' He lifted Angad like his mace and put him down on the other side. I was already walking away from them; they followed.

'Bali, a huge monstrous figure is on its way to Kishkindha,' I translated. 'Whoever this is, if he walks at his present speed, he would reach Kishkindha by tomorrow.'

I looked at Sugreev and then at Bali. We had been expecting this. There must be someone in the family of Dunduvi who would come for revenge. The herd must have seen him crossing the plains below and hurried back to the forest.

Do we have any evidence yet of this one being an enemy?' Bali asked.

'Yes,' I confirmed. 'The birds have heard him vowing to burn Kishkindha to ashes. He is coming to ...'

'To?' Ruma asked, irritated with the sudden restraint.

'Put an end to Bali?' Angad effortlessly said what I couldn't.

For a while, no one spoke. Even the leaves had stopped whispering. The spell lifted when we heard Bali cracking his knuckles.

'Kishkindha will be glad to welcome him,' a strange smile spread across his face. He looked cruel. 'I will break every bone of his and level him with the ground till his blood—'

'Bali!' I blurted out. 'There was once a man who never wanted to kill,' I reminded. 'He tried to make friends, even with the fiercest. He believed in winning hearts over losing lives.'

'That didn't work,' Bali got up and leapt forward. Sugreev and Angad went behind him.

Ruma kept her hand on my shoulder.

I could not tell her that Bali had started walking downhill. Changing for the better is hope. When a beautiful flower starts decaying, its rotten juice emits a pungent smell attracting the insects that will ruin it further. Danger was not a foreign creature advancing towards Kishkindha. Much bigger danger was seated as the unsettled anger of the king. Anger influences actions that are regretted later. Anger blindfolds. Anger burns intelligence to ashes.

*

In the morning, Angad woke up before Bali did. 'Father,' he asked innocently, shaking him. 'Many were saying yesterday that the monster approaching us is terrible and dangerous. Are you in danger?'

'What if I say yes?' Bali watched him keenly.

'Can I go in your place?' The boy left his father stunned. 'Kishkindha needs you more than me.'

Bali hugged his son. 'Kishkindha doesn't need anyone who is scared of danger.' He sat up and bent towards him. 'Listen, Angad. Never believe that your father is defeated, until you see him dead. Will you remember this?'

Large, glass-like hazel eyes turned misty. I pulled him towards me. 'Why do you say these things to him?' I pushed Bali with a leg and held the young one's face between my palms, as he fought back tears. 'Angad, even the next monsoon could bring danger. Storms may brew, and floods may surge. We don't call it danger because we know monsoons are inevitable. Whoever be the monster, it's only as bad as the monsoon. Your father will find a way out, like he always does.' He understood immediately and calmed down.

Bali shook his head in frustration. 'You are

turning him into a crybaby. He needs to grow up,' he said, stoking my ire further.

'May his father grow up first.'

*

The dry soil stirred up a storm by noon. Heavy footsteps assaulted the ground, his voice reverberating off the walls of Rishyamukh and echoing through the trees of Kishkindha. 'Bali! The wretched animal,' he screamed. 'Come face Mayavi. I will chop your body into parts and chew them into cud right here. My elder brother Dunduvi will then rest in peace.'

Seated beside me, Angad rushed out. I didn't stop him. Bali was already on his way. Sugreev followed. I uttered a prayer. Last night, when Angad was asleep, I had warned Bali. 'If this one is coming to avenge Dunduvi's killing, he is hungrier for victory than us. For he comes with a loss in his heart. He will try everything under the sun, including sorcery and treachery.'

'Good you mentioned treachery,' Bali yawned. 'The word gets my blood boiling. Won't subside until there is no one left to mourn Dunduvi.'

I sighed deeply. The war that Bali won against Dunduvi and the war he lost to Lali had stripped something important off him. Kindness. Empathy. Humility. The ability to choose peace. Bali had started to enjoy wars, taking pride in killing.

Mayavi was colossal. He must have endured days of rigorous physical training before setting out for Kishkindha. His laughter reached the clouds. 'This one wouldn't suffice for a morsel. But why do I fear when there is a tribe of monkeys to devour after sucking the bones of their king?' Mayavi reached for Bali, trying to lift him by the tail. Nothing moved. Angry now, he cursed and struck a mighty blow. A hand went up in defence. Another blow followed but was similarly repelled. The warring duo stood in a stalemate, their feet rooted to the ground, each pair of hands trying to push the other back. After what seemed like an entire day, Bali took a step forward. Mayavi retreated. Kishkindha cheered. Not only could Mayavi not proceed, but he also couldn't free himself from the vice-like grip of his opponent. An enormous kick landed on his belly, as Bali suddenly bounced up in the air and thrashed him against the banyan tree. Blood trickled down his head. Before he recovered, blows landed upon him one after the other, breaking his teeth and nose. Dishevelled, Mayavi managed to get up and run as fast as he could. With a tremendous war cry Bali chased the enemy, declaring that no leeway would be granted for him to come back healed, like the biggest mistake Kishkindha had made in the case of his brother. Mayavi and Bali disappeared from our sight. Angad dashed after them.

'Sugreev, go!' Ruma hissed. Terrified and shaking, Sugreev trailed behind Angad.

21

'Bali, what does the underworld look like?'

'Same as any other world, from the outside,' I was told. 'You wouldn't understand you are entering it. Anger revels there in the company of raging souls, fuelling the war of superiority.'

'Describe the entrance.'

'It resembled the mouth of a cave. Nothing extraordinary,' his voice drifted in. 'I didn't suspect a thing. Just instructed Sugreev to take care of Kishkindha as I jumped into the cave behind Mayavi.'

Inside the underworld, Mayavi's powers multiplied. With every blow dealt by Bali, another Mayavi sprang up wielding huge thorny clubs. Together, they attacked Bali. Little did he know that tricking Bali would be deadly. The king of Kishkindha fought alone with all his might, avenging the tears of Lali and the still stare of the dead fawn. Every time a row of Mayavis were defeated, a fresh line stood waiting a few steps deeper into the cave.

'He was luring you further inside,' I recollected.

'More than that,' Bali added. 'Mayavi was the son of a magical Asur architect. With each layer we crossed, Mayavi sealed the exit with sorcery. I ventured into the remote recesses of the cavity speedily, without stopping to check what was happening behind. Attacks rained down from unpredictable directions. Thorny clubs aimed for my head, cornering me towards the scorched edges of burning rivers. Storms hurled big boulders to crush me. One misstep would slash my body with the spiked leaves of sharp plants, colouring their surfaces in blood. Not a single moment of respite.'

I shivered once again, listening to the harrowing account. Bali had never been so descriptive during his lifetime. As he spoke now, I could see a cluster of images behind closed eyes. The uneven ground, known for the worst crimes underneath the soil, was claustrophobic, disconnected from nature by all means. Everything was artificial. All that energized Bali was missing. The sights, sounds, smell, feel – everything was distorted. Spine-chilling evidence of cruel and corrupt deeds adorned the horrifying walls as proud trophies – dilapidated remains of humans, animals, insects, birds, reptiles and plants. The underworld spared none.

'His strength dwindled after days of fighting …' Bali's voice continued.

Days! It was more than a year.

'… Mayavi started assuming smaller bodies – leopards with terrifying claws, rhinoceros with monstrous horns, antelopes with elongated canines, elephants with knotty trunks sashing the neck like a noose. When they fell, the thousand-hooded cobras bathed me in their venom. I felt like being pushed alive into my own pyre. Ten-mouthed spiders dropped from the top, biting wherever they could, leaving festering wounds that would fill with puss.'

Indra's son. Vayu's curse!

I could not help but wonder if Hanuman had suffered as much when the vajra of Devraj Indra had struck him on the chin! Revenge is never just retaliation; it always sets a higher benchmark. Whether between gods, humans or animals.

22

When Bali entered the cave, Angad had been sitting outside awaiting his father. Sugreev had come back to Kishkindha with words of hope: 'Bali will return soon.'

I had reclined into the banana forest, writing about my fears and anxieties, my faith and beliefs – and suppressing an urge to cry my heart out.

Time passed by. Sugreev returned to the mouth of the underworld again and again, each time returning with dwindling hope. Bali was untraceable. The dark hole had started to emit the fetor of the dead. Until, one day, a terrified gasp tore from his throat, his face drained of colour. A river of blood fountained out of the hellhole, staining everything in its way. Angad lay unconscious beside it. Assuming Bali to be dead, choking and wailing, overwhelmed by the loss, Sugreev had covered the mouth of the underworld with the largest rock and cemented the open pores with hard soil, cursing Mayavi to remain locked inside forever. He lifted Angad on his shoulder and carried him back to Kishkindha. Lives stopped. No one spoke a word. Birds gave up chirping, the deer stopped gossiping. The trees ceased to divulge their stories of endurance. I couldn't write.

Sugreev had gone straight to my father. Ruma and Father kept Angad in constant vigil. After two sleepless nights, he opened his eyes. My son lifted himself, unyielding to Ruma's coddling and cosseting to rest some more. He glanced at the silent crowd – their heads bowed in mourning, a hand or two sharing a touch of condolence. With eyes deep inside their sockets, he ran through the forest as fast as he could. Sugreev and Ruma kept calling out to him from behind. He dropped himself beside me in the banana forest and buried his face into my belly. I had hugged him back. Ruma halted at a distance, Sugreev came closer. 'I am still here, Angad.' He trembled, somewhat apologetic about the status. None of us answered. He waited and left eventually. Angad remained sitting, motionless.

'Mother, do you believe that Father is dead?' he asked.

'No,' I whispered.

He sat up. 'Then why don't you tell everyone?'

'It has been two years. Only Bali can prove that he is alive. We will have to wait.' I explained.

We held each other's hands and pledged to the eternal interlude, every day waking up with hope and sleeping with disappointment in the nights.

Not very long after, I found my son slapping a tree trunk with both hands. He used to do that as a child, when someone said something unacceptable about his father. The first time when he had gone berserk, he was no more than a year old. Anjani ma had ridiculed the king for staring at his wife while talking to Uncle Kesari.

Angad's silent protest got the monkeys to reveal their teeth, laughing their hearts out. Since then, Anjani ma would purposely say something against Bali to irk the grandson, and he would repeat the performance.

'Why are you stressed?' he shook off my hands rubbing his shoulder. 'Angad, I understand the obvious. What's new?' I prodded.

'Why don't you ever step out of this banana orchard?' he demanded, angrily. 'Do you know what is happening outside?'

If only I were interested. What would stepping outside accomplish? Seeing myself as a pitiful widow in everyone's eyes? Oh, no. How could I forget? I was supposed to witness worse than that.

One of those nights after Angad had slept off, I heard him walking into this part of the forest. 'Sugreev!' I sat up, surprised.

'Tara,' he seemed frightened. 'Ruma advised ...' he stammered, 'that you might need me. Now.' His face was lowered, refusing to look me in the eye, lest they slice him into pieces. 'Leave,' I could only say. He left immediately without a word and never returned.

I remained awake, my nights having become sleepless since Bali was proclaimed dead. The forest, once buzzing with life, had suddenly fallen into infinite quietude. Any movement felt like parched spirits lurking in the endless darkness. When the sun came up, Angad drifted closer to me.

'Mother, would you like me to sleep elsewhere?' He yawned.

'Don't grow up so fast, Angad,' I spoke with a stone face. 'And if you must, then use your brain.'

He pressed his cheek against mine and left. That evening, he returned with his fingers locked into a fist. 'Mother, don't fret over this,' Angad prefaced. 'They think, in the absence of Father, you have married Uncle Sugreev. They saw him entering the banana forest alone last night.'

I looked up at him. 'Did you fight with the tribe?'

'No,' he assured. 'It's not for me to clarify.'

My son had indeed grown up. He didn't tell

me how it hurt him, nor did he insult his parents by defending his mother before the undeserving. Just informed that Sugreev couldn't resist punching a few for their inordinate curiosity. But that wouldn't dispel the rumours or diminish their capacity to assume a connection.

When Ruma visited next, I shot a piercing glance at her. She was quite unaffected. 'Women need men, Tara, as much as men need women. Desires don't die with the death of the beloved,' she shrugged. 'Come back to life. You are rotting here like a stinking banana.'

I wanted to slap her. I wanted to hug her.

Why did Angad want me to step out of the banana forest? To meet whom, see what? In the eyes of the tribe, I wouldn't see myself as Bali's widow but as Sugreev's other wife! Angad slapped the tree trunk some more and sat down beside me.

'Uncle Sugreev enquires about you.' He stretched backwards. 'Often he walks me back until the edge of the forest but refuses to enter.'

'He is an old friend, Son. Very old. And very dear.' I remembered the good old days when relationships were spontaneous.

'The grass on the far end of the forest is growing,' he said, slowly and softly. 'Uncle Sugreev has ordered that the forest be cleared, and edible crops be farmed. Because tall grass is useless.'

'So?' I ignored the concern in his voice, though I knew where this was going.

'Uncle Sugreev has proposed planned farming,' he explained. 'Meaning, the pineapple and mango forests will be extended to multiply the fruit cultivation in every season. The excess will be traded off. Trade will enhance our relationships with foreign lands and natives, strengthening Kishkindha. Jambavan and Grandfather have given their consent.'

I remained calm, looking into the distance. With Bali absent, Sugreev had been made the king – a proposal made by my father, endorsed by Jambavan and Uncle Kesari and opposed by

Anjani ma. Sugreev had started taking charge of the forest.

'Stop running around the bush, Angad!'

'I overheard Uncle Sugreev discussing plans to catalyze miraculous fertilizers that could help yield more fruit crops. He wants the tribe to experiment with manufacturing preservatives so that the fruits would last longer. Aunt Ruma trashed the idea, but others seemed intrigued. He also wants to attempt hybrid planting. These are artificial techniques triggering overproduction. The soil and vegetation – both would suffer in the long run. Father would never have approved of these. He would be devastated by the felling of trees and clearing of the grass, whenever he returns.' Angad broke down.

I ran my hand over his back slowly, comforting him. 'It is fine, Angad. Bali had his own ways of working things out. Sugreev cannot do things like Bali. He is trying to do the best he can, for the benefit of Kishkindha.' I lifted his face between my palms. 'He is miserably trying to fit into a profound void left by Bali. But he can only speak the language he knows.' Angad looked at me with big tears fidgeting inside his large eyes. 'Help him as much as you can. Oppose him if you have enough reason. Convince him or get convinced. Work hard to make his decisions right, whatever they are.'

Angad was far from persuaded. He only nodded quietly, looking away, unwilling to argue. I nodded too, sadness overflowing from my eyes, wishing in my heart that he didn't give in so easily.

Since the tall grass had been cleared, many insects and reptiles migrated from their habitat to other ends of the forest. The original inhabitants were not happy, complaining of overcrowding because of alien breeds pretending kinship. Sugreev bore the brunt of the blame for jeopardizing their homes. Gossip, though, is the best leveller. The refugees asked the natives about the erstwhile queen of the land, once fiery and now silent, having engaged in an illicit affair with her brother-in-law. Friendships blossomed, folklore flourished. The natives opened their mouth to the refugees, mixing facts with fiction in proportions suited to the tastes of each storyteller. Some were so well conceived that the stories felt more real than the truth.

*

'What a fantastic, fertile land Kishkindha used to be,' Anjani ma lamented one day.

'You've said just what I have been thinking,' echoed Uncle Kesari. 'In very little time, the boy had turned this place into a surreal fantasy. Each ordinary animal was motivated to exhibit their unique talent. Kishkindha would be vibing with raw energy. That energy is lost now.'

'Everyone may have made peace with Sugreev, but they haven't forgotten Bali,' Jambavan agreed.

'They should never forget Bali,' Sugreev butted in tearfully. The elders fell silent, looking at each other, feeling both pain and helplessness. Sugreev sobbed alone. No one consoled him.

'I will erect a stone edifice in the grasslands on the southern edge of the forest,' he proposed once he was calmer. No one protested. 'A statue that touches the sky, inscribing the life and deeds of Bali on it, will inspire everyone through his indomitable legacy.'

The plan was soon put to action. Nal and Nil were entrusted with the task. Angad remained stoic. I heard the updates in snippets. Monkeys worked day and night, their euphoria about building the statue kept Kishkindha awake. Sitting at my usual place, I saw the stone monument steadily taking shape, raising its enigmatic head and erecting a formal entrance separating Kishkindha from the rest of the world. Duties were allotted to armed monkeys to report infiltrations should there be any. I tried to look away, but it was difficult. Nal and Nil's craftsmanship was extraordinary. Before long, the enormous statue of Bali stood tall, smiling back at the citizens of the land. How could I not stare at him, smile at him, and cry for him, hoping for my eternal wait to end for good. The statue appeared achingly real, as if it could move any time and make fun of us – having fallen for yet another prank. Maybe I'd chase him with a bamboo again and beat him into a pulp. Or should I hug him first and let the reserved tears find their release?

In my eagerness to see Bali again, I forgot that circumstances change personalities. The one who returned was not the husband I had been missing!

When the familiar voice roared from afar, I sat up with a jolt. The statue still looked the same, smiling affectionately at everyone. Then why did I hear a bitter howl? Resentful bellows tore through the morning sky again. Angad stood up too, a mix of excitement and fear shining in his eyes. Together, we rushed out of the banana orchard. Other animals emerged from other parts of the forest, all of us looking at the sky-high statue and moving towards it, trying to figure out the source of the voice.

A grotesque creature approached the edifice. It stopped in shock before the statue, until the guards tried to interrogate. The creature slapped them hard, howling as loudly as he could, his words incomprehensible. One of the guards fainted; another ran away. He entered the terrains unbarred. Lali rushed in with water and sprinkled some on the fallen monkey, rubbing his palms gently to bring him back to his senses.

'An enemy has entered Kishkindha,' he reported, shivering in despair, when he finally opened his eyes. 'I couldn't stop him. He must be somewhere inside, roaming in the forest. He is savage.' Marks on his cheeks clearly showed the finger impressions of the assaults he had sustained. I stared blankly, nothing entering my ears until Angad gently took my hands. His eyes were red, washed by tears. A faint smile crossed his lips. 'Looks ugly,' the guard added. 'Skin is ash black. Fur pulled out in places, flesh exposed. Head almost bare. Eyes swollen. Blood on the temple. Huge torso bent to the right, covered in bruises from head to tail. A beast straight from the abyss.'

I gazed at Sugreev. His erect body, the gleaming brown fur, the regal tail. The face of my Bali. I couldn't reconcile this image with what I was hearing. Angad started walking ahead; I followed him. From behind, Sugreev called out, 'Wait, take the mace.' He was holding his own weapon, clearly disturbed but trying to put on a brave face. Angad didn't look back. A mild storm swept through the terrain. The trees swayed left and right, dancing to their songs of resilience.

23

'Why did you stop?' I prodded.

'I thought you'd lost interest.'

'You didn't think that. You were waiting for the nudge.'

He chuckled.

'With a mace, you can hit a body. Not a swarm of flies. Mayavi launched a final attack. A cloud of gnats, with mouths like daggers, were biting my flesh. Their saliva poured acid onto the cuts, instantly burning the skin black. In the forest, your father used to amputate the afflicted body parts when someone came with such an infection. Large, green, dirty.'

Bali never called anything dirty. Whether it was the clear water of the Pampa or the rainwater collected in puddles where frogs croaked intermittently – he found everything beautiful. I bit my lips.

'I had no escape till I killed them all. Else the gnats would come out with me.'

'What did you do then?' I asked, straightening myself.

'Took the bites,' he said, 'while swiftly sloughing off the skin of a dead elephant nearby. I threw the peeled skin up into the air, trapped the enormous cloud within its folds and strangled them in one go. A few that still hovered were clapped between my hands. Mayavi was finished.'

I made a mental note to recount all of this to Angad. He should know Bali's war history down to the last detail. The story, however, was far from over.

'When I was finally free to look back for the first time since the war began, I saw ruins. Of bodies and a sea of blood,' the steady voice trembled. 'Picking up the mace and dipping my feet into the sticky floor, I started the return journey, unshackling myself from every closed layer by breaking open the countless spells sealing each entrance. It was worse than the war.'

'Why?' I was surprised.

'Each layer resembled a closed chamber with no trace of entrance or exit. I didn't know where to strike. Mayavi had left his weaponry to fight on his behalf when he was no more. In each of the layers, the key was different. A small, soundless spot was the point to hit in one. In another, it was the tiny chunk of ice that didn't melt in the heat. Yet another had a boiling pool at its rear end – I had to cross it and make my way into the next layer. It was endless. Exhaustive. Discovering the clues and breaking down the layers provided no joy because the next horrible layer was waiting to be conquered.'

Perhaps I could not even fathom how awful the journey must have been for Bali. I was crying, hitting my hand against the uneven ground, hurting myself, scratching the skin with my nails. Bali's trauma was way beyond anything I had ever known.

'I was alive. Breathing. Mayavi had arranged an everlasting revenge that made me want to die!' I had never heard Bali speak of his own death, not until the last day of his life. Why hadn't he told me all this before? 'More than once I considered jumping into the burning river and giving up. I somehow stopped myself and kept pushing.'

'Because you wanted to come back to us? Me and Angad?' I asked desperately. I needed to hear that, for once.

'No, Tara.' Bali was ruthless. 'I needed to put an end to Mayavi. Completely. Each remaining evidence of his intelligence needed to be destroyed.'

We both remained silent. My heart was beating loudly. Was Bali listening? I hugged myself, wrapping my arms around my body.

'Finally, I reached the mouth of the underworld. And ...' he paused.

I knew what this 'and' meant. A shapeless boulder had been clumsily placed there, its corners cemented with hardened earth. With one kick, Bali brought it down.

24

This was the first time in all these years that I observed notable changes in our familiar surroundings. Incessant monsoons had washed over Kishkindha this year. Parts of the forest with fallen trees were waterlogged. The adjoining lands were also affected. Many residents had to be rescued and resettled. There was a significant decline in the birds flocking to the trees. Some animals developed peculiar skin and stomach ailments – quite a few of which were infectious. Sugreev, in consultation with Father, chose for them an area where ginger plants grew in abundance. Monkeys didn't feed on such terrible vegetables. Thus, lesser footfall ensured lower chances of the infection spreading. This part of the forest was to be cleared, and the stems were to be bartered with kingdoms that were kind towards ginger. However, the plan was on hold until the monkeys recovered.

We spotted the militant near the edge of the ginger bed. Without a word of caution, the animals from this end attacked, their maces held high. Angad and I had no time to stop them. By the time we rushed in, a troupe of monkeys were sent hurtling and tumbling haphazardly in all directions like feathers in a storm. The creature was exposed once again amid the mayhem, the line of sight clear between him and me. Those cold hazel eyes froze.

'Bali,' I whispered. I couldn't tell whether he could hear me. Sugreev clonked behind us.

'Bali!' I called out again, louder this time. A frost of silence engulfed the forest. Those preparing to get up and charge again remained fallen, too numb to react.

'Tara...' He limped towards me. 'What have you done to yourself? What happened to you?'

Me! I hoped he wouldn't see his reflection in the waters of the Pampa anytime soon. I dragged myself forward; Angad held me tight so I wouldn't fall. We couldn't hug the man we loved most. He mirrored a tarnished stove, with roasted organs assembled into a body. Layers of grime clung stubbornly to the contours of his once-glistening muscles.

'What were you doing when I was away, dumb fellow?' Bali said to Angad. 'Why does your beautiful mother resemble a dried mango seed?'

We laughed. We cried. Soft sobs and hiccups joined us from behind. Bali glanced at Sugreev, his eyes more accusing than kind.

'Who placed the boulder to block the mouth of the cave, Sugreev?' Bali thundered without bothering to wait for pleasantries.

Boulder? Blocking the mouth of the cave? Angad and I looked at each other, shocked. Every eye was turned towards Sugreev.

'Blood fountained out of the mouth of the cave, Bali,' he fumbled. 'Outside, Angad had passed out. I thought you were ...' The brother wiped his tears. 'It had been more than two years. I sealed the mouth of the cave in the hope that Mayavi wouldn't be able to come out.'

Bali's eyes flickered like fire. He walked menacingly towards his sibling, with Sugreev stepping backwards. 'Didn't I warn that Mayavi was a master sorcerer? Didn't you know?' The voice was rising. 'He threw the first fruit and you gulped it down greedily?'

Something here was spiralling out of control. We needed to stop them before it was too late. Things were moving very fast, unveiling skeletons kept in the dark. 'Why were you so keen to declare me dead?'

The allegations left Sugreev stricken. He looked at Bali, bewildered, his voice lost. Distrust grew in the eyes of the onlookers.

'You wanted to be the king of Kishkindha? Was that why you betrayed me?' Bali was roaring now, like someone possessed. 'When you were a child, you loved to sit on top of the hill and imagine the peak to be your throne. What happened, Sugreev? The game was not over, or you never grew up?'

Not every allegation had a response. Some were met with a speechless void. Tears ran down the younger monkey's eyes. He forgot to defend himself.

'What have you done to Kishkindha?' Bali howled. 'The trees displaced, the suffering animals expelled. You are worse than a human!' he pointed at the ailing monkeys confined in the ginger grove. 'And you harassed Tara with your lies?'

Amid the horrible drama unfolding in the open, a voice from the crowd blurted out, 'Tara is Sugreev's wife now.'

There was no better fuel for this fire. Bali stiffened, his eyes turning red with unprecedented wrath. 'Should I pluck the criminal brain off your body, or should I break your neck?' His fingers closed into tight fists and the biceps, way leaner than Sugreev's, shook in anger.

Sugreev fell on his knees, without a consideration for his usurped position. Yesterday's king had hit the ground. 'I can explain everything. Don't accuse me of treachery. I am not a traitor.' He joined his hands, seeking mercy, weeping profusely.

Bali kicked him with his wounded leg. 'How many of your betrayals should I pass off as coincidences?' His bellow reached every corner of the forest. 'What were you conspiring against Tara? You didn't? Then how dare the monkeys call her your wife? Why?' He slapped Sugreev as hard as he could. He lowered his voice suddenly, cornering his brother with unsteady, hostile steps. 'Now I understand ...' Forceful blows landed on the younger twin's back. 'Your role models have trapped *her* too, inside some dark and daunting cave and closed its mouth with a boulder which the poor woman cannot break through.' Slaps, kicks and punches fell one after the other. Sugreev wriggled in pain and insult, but did nothing to stop Bali. We stood around like puppets, overwhelmed by the shocking turn of events. 'Tell me where they have confined *her*. Tell me. Tell me. Tell me now.'

Bali seemed to have lost all good sense, deriving brutal pleasure in hurting his twin, unwilling to hear any justification from the bruised and yeilding defendant. Mayavi may have died, but Bali fought like he was still not done with the confrontation. He lifted a rock to smash his brother's head. I jumped in between, bringing him to a sudden halt.

'Move away, Tara. You don't know what he has done,' Bali commanded.

Never had his voice sounded so harsh. The man I had married was lost somewhere, deep in the maze of the underworld. The one who emerged victorious mimicked the vanquished. Hateful, murderous, merciless, fierce, vile.

I looked straight into Bali's eyes with disdain. The aggression reduced drastically. He threw the rock aside.

'Take Sugreev away from Kishkindha. For a while. Until we restore the balance here. Help him recover in peace,' I commanded, gesturing to Jambavan.

Lali had already come forward to help Sugreev, casting resentful glances at the elder monkey. 'Inflicting violence upon the meek to hide your inefficacy?' She hissed as she held Sugreev up, who was on the verge of passing out. 'The curses are stacking up,' she threatened. 'You will be punished.' I glared at her, she looked away.

Bali paid no heed to her words and shouted at Sugreev. 'Run, run to save your skin, you fool. That's what you have done all your life. Hiding like a coward. Go wherever you like. Just know that if you ever step back in Kishkindha, your former protector will peel the skin off your body. This is my promise to you. Go, hide.'

Angad and I stood between them, witnessing identical scenes unfold on two ends. Here, Bali was limping away from us, injured and defiant. There, the shattered, breathless Sugreev was being carried away. Everyone dispersed slowly, too shaken to deliberate on these developments. Other than Jambavan and Lali, no one followed Sugreev. It had been a very long time since the younger monkey had ruled Kishkindha.

Couldn't he inspire anyone to love him? Why was he accompanied by only two today – one at my insistence and another who hated Bali for personal reasons? Where were Sugreev's own followers?

Angad looked at me, and I at him.

'I will go after your father. You find Ruma.'

'No!' replied Angad, surprising me. 'We must do the opposite.'

I took a moment to appraise the young face before me. We set off in opposite directions.

*

The news had reached Ruma faster than it came to me. She was packing concoctions and ingredients for Father with deadly calm. My eyes met Father's, we both chose silence. With great restraint, I waited for Ruma to finish her chores and for Father to leave.

'What are you doing here?' We both asked each other.

'Ruma,' I tried again. 'Why are you not with Sugreev?'

'The doctor has gone to attend to him,' she assured, as if she was talking about a regular patient. 'Move from there and pass the neem leaves,' Ruma instructed. 'I must prepare the disinfectants for Bali.'

There was no anger in her voice; she was weirdly composed.

'Ruma, wake up,' I pleaded. 'Sugreev needs you now.' I wanted to cry. She glanced at me, perhaps measuring my present status. Was this the former queen or a childhood friend? I leapt forward, holding her closer to me, my palm caressing her head.

'Has the king exiled me too?' she asked softly. My hand stopped; I shuddered under her penetrating gaze.

'No.' I let my tears flow.

'Then I am not going anywhere.' She freed herself from my rigid embrace. Looking at my baffled face, she smiled. 'Remember those days, Tara, when we were not married? The twins had just landed here from nowhere, and Kishkindha wasn't Kishkindha yet.'

How could I forget? Who would forget? Those memories were all we had now. I had easily befriended Sugreev. Bali was an attractive yet distant enigma. Ruma was Father's favourite though I was his daughter. She chased daily goals, I chose freedom.

'I was in love with Bali. Bali was not. He told me to marry Sugreev. I obeyed. You know why?' Her choking voice snaked all over me as she bared herself. 'Obedience was the only expression I was left with to convey my devotion to Bali. I moulded into a faithful wife, making my husband happy in every way, just as Bali would have wanted me to. Not for a day did I derail from my commitment. But obedience was my dissent too. Everything I had ever done was for Bali.'

Stripped of words, I dropped to the ground, unable to move or convince Ruma to rethink. She dismissed my dilemma. 'This is not your battle, Tara. It is about Sugreev's truth. I will be his soldier today. My presence in Kishkindha will shower the king with spears of guilt, distressing him far more than the suffering of my innocent husband today.'

Some protests did not follow a traditional script. Was Bali capable enough, in his present state, to read through Ruma's rebellion? Doubtful. Nal came with news. Lali had taken Sugreev to Rishyamukh. Father had reached there. I nodded sadly. Good decision. It was the only place Bali couldn't visit.

*

On the other end of the forest, Angad was struggling. Bali was agitated, burning with fever. He refused to eat or rest. He was determined to return the forest to its indigenous splendour. As a first step, he wanted the gateway dismantled. The craftsmanship went unnoticed; he saw the boundaries it had pronounced. And he found Sugreev's statue standing with its head held high! Half unconscious, he kept kicking in the air envisaging the demolition, all the while muttering to himself. 'This is how they entrap. *She* must have been cast out like the ailing monkeys, isolated like a disease. He knew everything but didn't alert me. How could he? What an unimaginable deceit! How could I not see this earlier?' He slapped himself. The swelling on his forehead aggravated further with the careless strike.

'Bali,' I called out, unsure of what I was to say next. He looked at me – troubled, vulnerable, lonely, unwell. 'Sugreev is not corrupt. Please stop.'

The words fell on deaf ears. 'He made stupid assumptions. He concealed facts. Callously and irresponsibly, as he always does,' Bali countered.

'He meant well, I am sure. He never intended harm. He cannot—'

'Fools always cause trouble. Intentionally or otherwise,' my reasoning was rejected. 'Good riddance.'

'Mother—' Angad interrupted. We both turned. Bali recoiled as if he had seen a ghost. He gathered himself into a bundle and turned over the other side, unwilling to look at the visitor ushered in by Angad.

Ruma acted as if nothing had happened. 'Stick to watermelon, banana, pomegranate and papaya. Begin feeding dates and peaches after three days. The strength will start building back. Avoid nuts for now. No pineapples, tomatoes or grapefruits. They might cause stomach aches. Here is a mixture of guava and pumpkin seeds for brain strength. Needs to be administered right away,' she advised.

Bali didn't confront Ruma. Meekly, he followed her instructions and swallowed the medicines. Within a few moments, he was flat on the ground, sleeping and snoring.

'Datura,' she explained. 'He won't get up until tomorrow morning.'

Punishing me further for my incompetence, Ruma left. Angad and I were worn out, our heads reeling with a thousand thoughts. I heard him saying, 'Mother, you stay here. I will go and check on Uncle Sugreev.'

He leapt away.

25

A few days ago, an earthquake had devastated the forest. Trees had fallen, blocking the paths and destroying some bird nests. It left fissures in some parts. The water of the Pampa rose high up in the air and fell with a terrible splash. No significant loss of life was reported. But the tremors blew a wave of uncertainty among the inhabitants. I had an inkling that something was happening somewhere.

'Bali, why didn't you ask me anything when the tribe called me Sugreev's wife?' My forehead arched. The banana leaves swayed in the air.

'What, woman?' Bali rebuked. 'Can't your idle brain sniff anything better than stale bananas?'

'Don't change the topic,' I warned.

'Why me?' he countered. 'Ask the owls. Even your worst haters wouldn't believe that you could have had anything to do with the younger twin.'

'So ruthlessly you accused him of all kinds of sins. Why?' I asked sadly. 'Just because he made some changes in Kishkindha that didn't match your vision? It was only a misunderstanding that led him to close the mouth of the underworld!'

The cold air carried the smell of lavender, soothing my nerves. It was as if I felt Bali's touch. 'The conflict was elsewhere, embedded deep within, which we both consciously ignored. It assumed a form in my absence,' Bali analysed. 'Back in Kishkindha, I saw a different individual with independent thoughts. Struggling, but emerging from the underconfident brother I had known. I felt disowned.'

'Disowned!' I cried out. 'How?'

'We both were the sons of nature, Tara. We grew up amid its generosities and deformities. Yet, our ideologies diverged,' Bali sounded unbearably serene. 'At a transformational juncture, I remained stuck to the tradition of the vanar – the monkeys that submitted to nature. Sugreev was rapidly evolving into a 'van-nar' *– forest-dwelling humans attempting to reform nature.'*

I kept quiet. Bali was making a very difficult confession. If he were alive, he would never have said this. Death detaches souls from many awkward burdens.

'He had moved on,' Bali's voice rang again. 'I smelt of a passive insurgence that had grown steadily for long, and manifested when I was no longer a hindrance.'

'He handed over all reins the moment you returned,' I reminded him desperately. 'He was willing to step behind.'

'It was not the same anymore. Not for me,' Bali lamented. 'Once a war begins, you are dragged into a cycle of cruelty, with or without your consent. When the deer was killed, everything changed. The pressure of failure was enormous.' We both remembered the gruelling times, brimming with tension. 'If you wax, you will wane too,' Bali continued. 'Everything that grows will eventually wilt. The phase of growth is always inspiring. Very few can retain the same grace during their falling phase. I failed there again, miserably.'

Another gust of lavender-scented air swept through the fur on my skin – bundled and dusty. I tried to trap the air within my fist, it escaped.

'Don't be sad for me, Tara. Feel happy for Sugreev,'

Bali tried to cheer me up. 'He will be remembered, celebrated, worshipped.'

How could I feel happy for Sugreev? Was happiness so precious that it had to come with the death of a dear one? Was Sugreev happy now? Of course not, he was shattered. I felt a lump in my throat. How beautiful were the times when the brothers walked together on this soil, smiling and differing with each other. Energetic Bali, sulking Sugreev ...

'See how you remember him,' Bali pointed out, reading my mind instantly. 'The pensive one, disagreeing in silence.' I refrained from talking, only wiping my tears.

'Our lives were so entwined that we both couldn't flourish at the same time,' Bali reasoned. 'Sugreev was eclipsed by me. I had a majestic run. It was Sugreev's turn to shine. I had to fade.'

Logic falls in place. Emotions don't. Crusaders always paid the ultimate price. The conformists survived.

'Is Sita back in Ayodhya?' I asked suddenly, remembering the other crusader I had known. Bali didn't answer. I coaxed him to tell me the truth.

'She is no more,' I was told the unthinkable.

'She gave birth to twin boys at Maharishi Valmiki's hermitage. Time brought them to a battle with their own army from Ayodhya. The boys defeated their uncles in war. When they discovered the ancestry of the young warriors, they were brought back to the palace of Ayodhya along with their mother. The people showered her with the fire of doubts, once again. This time, Sita refused to humour their intrusion. She seized from them the licence to question her.'

'How?' I could not hear myself; my heart had stopped beating.

'She called upon Mother Earth and slipped inside her womb. Forever,' Bali offered to my battered faith. Dreadful were the designs of destiny.

'Ram did nothing to stop her?' I wondered aloud.

'When has Ram ever stopped her?' Bali sounded surprised. 'He has always accepted all her wishes. Sita had called for renunciation. She rejected every relationship that suspected her integrity. As the ruler of such rogues, along with the righteous in the country, the king accepted this punishment.'

I cringed. 'Hope Sita's conspirators are satisfied now.'

'They are out of work. It took them days and months

to paint Sita as unfaithful and persuade more people to believe in their theories. With one stroke, she has destroyed their vanity and shamed everyone else who stood watching.'

I could imagine the people Bali described. All crooks looked alike.

'So many battles and so much bloodshed – all for the togetherness of a few days, followed by a lifelong estrangement?' Resentment seethed in my heart. If Ram was godly, why couldn't he grant a longer life to Bali and honour to Sita? Who could answer me? Who was answerable to me? What was the answer?

'Calm down, Tara,' Bali said, distraught in another world just as I was, sitting in the forest of Kishkindha. 'Ram and Sita are celestial companions. They did not come to the earth to walk hand in hand throughout their lifetime.'

The winds ceased blowing. Birds muted their songs. Nature was gloomy. Or perhaps, they were all equally curious to know more.

'Fervid attachment can distract leaders from their duty. Love might entice them to favour individual rights over collective prosperity,' my husband said, his

words measured and punctuated with pauses to ensure I understood properly. 'If you are truly dedicated to leadership, you must be willing to detach and let go. Your object of love could be dragged away to set you free. It's a cosmic secret.'

Secret! Not a simple one but a cosmic secret. I wish I could celebrate the possession.

'The godly and their devotees will lose their dearest ones. Togetherness doesn't end, only dependence ceases. You hear me?'

When Bali was alive, he would caress my hair and stroke my shoulders as he spoke like this. I could feel the urgency in his words even now, in the absence of his touch. 'Ram separated from Sita, by that cosmic command. Sugreev lost me. It was all interconnected.'

Sugreev. The twin brother. He befriended Ram, I didn't. Yet suffering had befallen both of us who loved Bali most. Despite the miscalculation, I still had access to Bali. Sugreev did not. Mesmerizing was the balance sheet maintained by the celestial accountants.

Closing my eyes, I silently wished Sita well, wherever she may be. 'What next?' I inhaled deeply, the air reaching my lungs.

'The good people of Ayodhya will lose their king. With Sita gone, the Ramayan draws to an end. Ram has nothing left in his story. He will forsake the world and unite with her. Narayan will go back to his Lakshmi. The withdrawal has begun.'

Bali mourned the great loss of a country which was about to lose its beloved king, after being abandoned by their resolute queen. He harboured no animosity against Ram. I was not as generous.

'Was it the day of the earthquake that Sita left?'

'Yes,' Bali confirmed.

26

With Bali's return to the forest, Kishkindha was slowly settling back to its old rhythm. As winter approached, the animals began to slow down. The herons and saras loitered aimlessly before flying away. Every night, Ruma poured turmeric and medicinal herbs into the Pampa. When Bali bathed in its waters each morning, the therapeutic water would wash his body. Later, Ruma and I would dive into the lake to filter it, sanitizing the water for others. The Pampa had witnessed us playing and splashing at each other in our childhood. We used to hold each other's heads underwater and released only after the penalty felt befitting for the quarrel we'd had. The lake would respond to our banter, with ripples and froth along its banks. It wasn't accustomed to the silence between us today. The water now maintained serene respite, tamed to our purpose and cooperated without being asked. Every day when we left the lake after our cleansing routine, it heaved a sigh of relief.

Bali was recovering fast. He had not yet resumed his flight across the world during his early morning prayers. But his complexion was returning to normal, the bruises and the cuts had dried and his fur was growing back. He was sleeping soundly. His lost appetite was back after many days of warring without food and water. He had started visiting different corners of the forest, asking after the well-being of all, noting down tasks that required attention, meeting the elders, playing with the newborns and lending a hand in chores – to whoever needed help. His training for the children with mace and wrestling had also begun. I accompanied him.

'Hey,' I would demand. 'I want to teach this posture. Get back.'

Panting and tired but unwilling to admit it, Bali would stand with his hands on the waist. 'Why?'

'Ah! It is my favourite,' I would quip and take over, sending the monkey to rest.

My favourite move. My favourite posture. My favourite weapon. My favourite learner. My favourites intervened in Bali's coaching whenever he seemed uncomfortable but was too proud to let it be known.

Sugreev visited often, seeking forgiveness. When he came for the first time, he stood speechless at the sight of the demolished edifice. The fondly constructed idol had been perceived as Sugreev's attempt to display his power and displace his twin. Even Bali could not recognize himself!

Each time, Sugreev was turned away. He left pleading and weeping. Father had managed to heal his body, but his mind still bore the scars of

Bali's pitiless allegations, reiterated and revived on every opportunity. Once, when Sugreev refused to leave, Bali chased him with his mace, hitting his brother and threatening to throw him into a dark cave from where his voice would never be heard again.

'I have done no such thing,' Sugreev shouted while running away to save his life.

'You withheld vital information at an important time,' Bali accused, hurling his mace at him.

Sugreev dodged it, but not without injury. He collided against a rock and crawled in pain, holding his bleeding foot. 'It was scary. I was afraid that ...' He gasped, dropping his leg back to the ground before leaping ahead.

'If you weren't a fool, *she* would be here today. You robbed her life,' Bali howled back, running after him till the younger twin reached the slopes of Rishyamukh.

He panted while standing still, turning to face Bali. 'You are depriving me of my home and everything else that is rightfully mine. This is unfair.'

Bali, standing where he was, mocked Sugreev's cowardice and shouted imprecations. He abused Rishyamukh for shielding him.

*

This continued for days. Their conflict had become a ritual now. The parrots flying over the forest gleefully whistled the king's name. Everyone could sympathize with Bali's anger; Sugreev's helplessness went without any representation. Initially a few tried to reason. They were shouted down and advised to leave for Rishyamukh if Kishkindha felt unsuitable. Slowly, the questioning voices died out. Conscience of the masses made peace with the popular opinion. No one wanted to name their child Sugreev. In every other family, a newborn was called Bali.

'Angad,' I whispered one day. 'What on earth is happening here?'

He looked around before responding. 'Not every time is the right time to speak, Mother,' he whispered back. 'Sometimes we must stand and watch, and wait for the time to pass.'

'Every day is imprinting its consequences,' I lamented. 'It will bring suffering to all.'

'Father won't understand. He is dealing with internal demons. Until he finds peace, he wouldn't stop seeing a demon in his brother.' He patted my hand. 'Uncle Sugreev is aware of it; we have spoken. The weight of the past that cannot be changed is sitting too heavily on the present.'

I shivered. 'What do you know about their past?'

'Just what I told you. Not a thing more.' The conversation ended there.

*

Ruma sometimes took walks at night, maybe to feel the breeze or to ease the disquiet of loneliness. Angad went to see her every evening and spent the night there, on the pretext of feeling too sleepy after a heavy meal. Once he slept, she set out to explore the forest on her own, revisiting spots filled with memories. She never entered the banana grove where Bali and I rested. One night, after she passed by, Bali sat up.

'Why doesn't she go to Sugreev?' He shook my arm.

'You didn't sleep?' I refused to answer him.

He paid no attention to my sarcasm. 'You talk to her. Persuade her to go to Rishyamukh.'

'I tried. She said she'll decide whether to stay or leave her own land, unless forced by the king.'

Bali turned sides. The silence had never felt so deafening.

After spring had unfurled its colours on the terrain, warm summer months brought the abundance of far-stretched azure skies with cotton clouds floating by. Children played for long hours, wiping their sweaty necks, while adults slept late, indulging in endless conversations on balmy moonlit nights. The breeze swayed the buds at their whims. Big trees rejoiced the resemblance of fluttering young leaves with their fallen ancestors. Fireflies flocked around until the sun shone brightly in the mornings. Fruits and vegetables chose their corners, where the soil was suited to the demands of the roots. The wildflowers had tantrums of their own, sprouting wherever they found space, climbing up the mango tree trunks and running over the base of the banana, spreading horizontal and vertical veils with tiny leaves surrounding the yellow, orange, purple, red and white blooms. Butterflies left their larva to be cocooned into more butterflies, and cuckoos couldn't stop singing.

Amid such celebration one day, we heard Sugreev standing at the entrance of Kishkindha, challenging Bali for a duel. 'I have had enough, Bali. I waited as long as I could, hoping that you would understand. Alas, not everyone appreciates patience. I will not stay in hiding any longer. I have returned to reclaim the position that is rightfully mine.'

I stood up with a jerk. The voice was undoubtedly Sugreev's, but it seemed someone else had entered his body to make him say such things. My chest pounded. I climbed up a tree to inspect. There he stood with a mace on his shoulder. He was really inviting Bali for a duel. The sunlight fell directly on his face, his mane shining. Unusual energy radiated from him. The fear that sat upon his face like a second skin was missing. He looked handsome.

Footsteps below the tree made me look down. Bali had heard him too. He was gathering his mace, gritting his teeth, his jaws tightening. I jumped down to land before him and blocked his way.

'What, woman? Step aside. Save your jokes for a more opportune hour,' Bali dismissed, irritated.

'Don't go, Bali,' I remained where I was. 'Don't fight with Sugreev today. It is a trap.'

Bali looked at me, shocked. 'Don't go! And let the world think I am afraid of this idiot's odd challenge? Have you lost your mind, Tara?'

'Not a single ant in Kishkindha or beyond would think so. Everyone knows ...' I couldn't complete my sentence.

'Every little event can change perceptions,' Bali cut me short. 'They know Bali is strong. But Bali shirking from a challenge would put a dent that faith. Doubts will rise inside their heads, trust will suffer. What makes you so frightened suddenly?' he gestured for me to make space.

I fumbled. 'Angad goes to Rishyamukh sometimes.'

'I know that. So?' Bali stood with his hands crossed over his chest. 'Don't look so shocked. Tell me what is brewing.'

'Ram, the exiled prince of Ayodhya, was crossing Rishyamukh with his brother Lakshman. His wife, Sita, has been kidnapped by Ravan, your friend from Lanka. They met Hanuman and Sugreev. The four have joined hands to attack Lanka. Sugreev is slowly gathering his own army. This could lead to a major war,' I shared the news from a few days ago which I had kept to myself, wondering how to broach this with Bali. I did advise him to call Sugreev back. It had been a very long time for the twin to stay away. Bali had got up and left the banana forest in response to my unsolicited counsel, unwilling to discuss further.

'Two people?' He waved two fingers before me now. 'Joined Sugreev? One missing woman. Ravan is the enemy. Ram, Lakshman, Sugreev.

Fine, let's add Lali, Hanuman and Jambavan. That's an army?'

The way he broke the information into split portions, it sounded ridiculous. Only if it was as simple. 'Ram is said to be an incarnation of Lord Vishnu. It is not a joke. Process the information with due diligence.'

Sugreev shouted again. 'What happened, Bali? Have you gone into hiding? What is taking you so long? If you are not fit for a fight today, I will be back tomorrow. Tell me.'

'You hear that?' Bali's face was turning red with anger.

'No, you hear that,' I lashed back, equally angry. 'Do you think Sugreev will ever talk to you like this? He is clearly instigated. Some human – I don't know possessing what powers and intending what – is taking advantage of a squabble between brothers. Are you blind?'

Bali put his hands on my shoulders, drawing me closer. 'That is why it is important to show the human his place and the brother his.' His grip tightened. 'If Ram is God, he would not need Sugreev's support. If Ram is wise, he would approach Bali with impressive records in wars, leading a forest full of denizens trained for situations known and unknown. He wouldn't seek out a loser who hasn't killed a mouse, couldn't win over the hearts of those he ruled for more than two years.' Removing his hands, he lifted the mace. He looked at me for one last time before leaping away. 'And finally, decide who is Sugreev for you. Is he innocent or wicked? Is he someone who has been punished unfairly by a cruel brother? Or is he a scoundrel conspiring against his dear ones with the help of a man who could be a god? The clarity will be good for you.'

Bali left with long strides. My foot shaking with each step, I followed him. I kept praying. My heart missed several beats. Bali didn't say a single word in response to Sugreev's unusual taunts. He just proceeded with the mace on his shoulder. By then, a lot of people had gathered to enjoy the spectacle. Who would pass such an opportunity for entertainment? It would inspire more jokes, spawn more gossip and give rise to more offensive phrases. 'As tearful as Sugreev' had become quite popular of late.

*

The duel ended sooner than I had expected. After the initial enthusiasm, Sugreev seemed to have lost interest. A few blows landed on his head and shoulder; another kick brought him to his feet. Sugreev was not afraid like before, but he was not taking the fight seriously either. Bali jumped up in the air to fall over him. He rolled aside. By the time the elder twin had hit the ground and got up with a hand raised to strike, Sugreev hobbled away towards Rishyamukh, leaving Bali gritting his teeth and the cheerleaders laughing.

Bali kept looking at the path to Rishyamukh, long after Sugreev was gone. When he turned, he found me staring.

'What now?' he tried to stroll past me as if this were routine.

I blocked his way. 'You noticed Sugreev has changed, didn't you? This wasn't the silly twin overshadowed by his elder brother. Answer me.'

'Good for him,' Bali said dismissively. He got up and leapt from branch to branch, heading towards the banana forest.

Not letting him off this easily, I gave a chase. The monkey was playing games; he enjoyed my rants when I was angry. How would I explain to him that this was not the time for fun? There he was. I found his tail hanging and spanked it with a fallen branch. Nothing changed. Two bananas fell on my head.

It was not his tail, just a muddled rope tied with bananas to mislead me.

'Bali!' I shouted at this untimely prank, searching for him between the trees. He was giggling from some hidden corner. 'Come out, right now.' I hunted impatiently, waiting to slap him right across the face. A bunch of banana flowers showered from above. I looked up immediately. No one. Gathering the flowers inside my hand – I kept biting, chewing and swallowing hastily to calm my nerves. A mild dust storm blew over my eyes, dry soil whirling up in the air along with brown leaves. I sat there, frustrated, my tail coiled on the ground. After counting upto six deep breaths I sprang straight up, pulling the big monkey out of the tree from where he was preparing to launch yet another prank. Holding him mid-air, our eyes locked. So many years had passed between us. Bali was elegant in his prime, the spark in his hazel eyes as seductive as the day when he first looked at me. Who would believe this body had withstood the onslaught of unforgiving ferocity, this mind had battled multiple traumas! The face was flirtatious, tempting and mischievous. One smile from Bali could still fix a world of uncertainties. A little attention from him made me blush. We were steadily falling to the forest ground. He manoeuvred to position himself beneath me. His back hit the ground first; I landed on top of him.

The fallen leaves of the forest gathered fast to make for a cosy bed. He wasted no time in sealing my mouth with his. Carnal desires overtook everything else. We couldn't take our hands off each other. Our bodies ached, the hearts yearned for more. The throbbing sensation between our legs blurred the difference between day and night. Exhausted, we fell asleep holding each other close. We woke up to make love again, then drifted back to sleep in each other's arms. Bali was insatiable, and so was I. Not every day called for such a divine union. I adjourned our conversation for another day.

Little did I know, that day would never come.

27

The morning began beautifully. Bali planted a firm kiss on my lips before leaving for the Pampa. I lingered a while longer, savouring the touch on my neck, shoulder and waist. Mid-day, when the sun was high in the sky, Sugreev returned.

'Come out, Bali. We left our duel incomplete yesterday. Let us finish the game. I am prepared. Are you?'

A chill ran down my spine. I hadn't expected him to return so soon. Bali was nowhere near me. I leapt to a spot from where I could see him. The sight in front jolted me to the core. Red kumkum was smeared on Sugreev's forehead. He wore a garland of marigold around his neck. I had never seen the brothers indulging in such accessories. Why today? What motivated Sugreev to craft a visual distinction from his brother? It couldn't be a mere fancy; there had to be more to it. My heart sank. My worst fears were coming true. From afar, I saw Bali walking ahead. Howling and panting, I ran towards him. Between us, a crowd of laughing hooligans had gathered again for a repeat of show from the previous day. Halted abruptly, I leapt above them. Bali had already reached the edge.

'Don't, Bali. For my sake, don't go. Stop for once,' I shouted at the top of my voice. The cheer of the crowd drowned my plea, but Bali turned. He flashed a serene smile and dashed away, ignoring all my attempts to prevent the futile duel. The twins began with a war cry. Tears streamed down my face as I dropped myself to the ground, folding my hands, praying for mercy. Angad rushed to my side, trying to comfort his harrowed mother.

Bali and Sugreev locked hands, each trying to overthrow the other. Sugreev seemed better prepared than the day before, shining with a lustre. His eyes gleamed with a saintly panache – spirited and fearless. In contrast, Bali appeared playful. He picked up Sugreev and hurled him far, amidst encouragement from the crowd. The younger twin put a leg forward, bringing Bali down and climbing on top of him, only to be sent flying with one blow from his elder brother. The intensity of the fight heightened. Unlike other occasions, they fought like equals. Sugreev relentlessly attempted to corner Bali. Bali was not giving him a single chance to do so. Bali treated him like a toy, Sugreev proved his resilience again and again. Punches and kicks landed in abundance. The audience shivered, chattered and shifted uncomfortably. Every strike seemed life-threatening, yet both combatants escaped the claws of death and sprang up to launch the next attack. After a thrilling hour, they picked up their maces.

As the fight reached its peak, the twins jumped high in the air. Bali made a swift turn and planted a resounding blow on Sugreev's chin. The latter winced in pain but refused to yield. He soared up instead with a howl, preparing to return the gesture, raising his mace above his head. That is when, from behind one of the bushes, a terrific lightning flashed. Bright and blinding. I crashed to the ground, closing my eyes shut. Animal instincts seldom fail.

For the next few moments, no one could see anything. We only heard the roars of the twins hidden in the enclosure of the magnificent radiance. A deafening explosion reverberated through the forest, silencing everyone present. Every heart forgot to beat. One of the two voices started mellowing down. The luminance was fading out. Through the haze appeared two blurry figures. One high above, holding his mace with both hands. The other outstretched horizontally below, sinking downwards.

Bali descended like the uprooting of a colossal tree, cracking the earth's surface. His mace fell and rolled away, sending waves of shock through the terrain.

Sugreev landed behind him, watching in disbelief. The mace dropped from his hand as well. He rushed towards his twin. 'Bali, get up,' he shouted. 'We are not finished yet, we can't be. Get up, Bali. We need to continue the duel.' He took his brother's hand in his trembling ones. 'How could you do this? Why did you do this?' He wailed. 'You always said that you wouldn't encourage treachery. What was this? Why?'

Angad left me with my weak knees and sped forward. Sugreev collapsed onto Bali, looking utterly destroyed. From behind the bush, two humans emerged – one dark-skinned and another fairer. One calm, the other fidgety. Sugreev turned towards the dark-skinned male, hands folded together. 'Do something, help us. Punish me, spare my brother. Take back your arrow, Sri Ram, return my Bali.' He wept.

Bali had began counting his breath. He gazed at Angad, searching for something.

'Where is your mother?' he asked, coughing out blood. I hurled myself towards him, unsure if there was any ground left beneath my feet. Before Bali breathed his last, he looked at me and demanded the impossible.

*

A few days had passed since we cremated Bali on the banks of the Pampa. Dark smoke rose up in the air from his pyre, reducing his body into ashes. The body I had made love with, only a few hours ago. The smoke travelled northwards, just like Bali leapt each morning during his prayers. I stared at it for as long as I could. Even as Bali left the world, he was perhaps making one last trip to look for the woman he had searched for all his life!

Nothing entered my ears any longer, I could see no one. Tears cloaked the soil of Kishkindha, the inhabitants engulfed by regret and fear. Ram kept his face down, his eyes meeting mine only once. No words were exchanged.

I walked alone through the forest, visiting the places we frequented as a couple, almost watching ourselves gravitating into each other in the recent past. At the edge of the datura bed, I stopped. This was where our story had begun. I stood there, feeling slightly drowsy. The datura flowers bowed their heads in grief. One hand landed on my shoulder. Angad hugged me tight, unwilling to let go, and forced me out of there.

I retreated into a confinement, sparingly coming out to fulfil certain duties. The duties that Bali had assigned to me as his last wish. The monsoon winds were on their way. The tribe was preparing themselves to accompany Ram for the great war against Lanka, post the rains. Sugreev's tribe. Within a few days, they would begin the journey southwards. They would have to cross the ocean and reach the island where Sita was being held captive. Nal and Nil had started thinking of possible ways to build a bridge on the ocean surface, for the soldiers to travel. Other than Hanuman and Bali, no one was skilled to fly across the ocean. The ground on which I sat was wet. The drizzles competed with my tears in vain. And Sugreev's too. He had entered the banana forest some time back. I heard him sobbing but refused to acknowledge it. He remained crouched in the corner. I expected him to leave. He didn't. The night passed.

'What do you want?' I asked before daybreak.

'I thought you would want me dead.' He pointed at Bali's mace lying beside me. Men take strange liberties.

'If I wanted to smash your head, I would have done so before cremating Bali.' My eyes were still burning with the heat of the pyre. 'Wouldn't have waited for you to make yourself available on a dark, desolate night.'

'I didn't mean that, Tara.' He looked downwards like a convicted criminal, his voice drenched in agony. It was difficult for him to stand before me, but he couldn't avoid it either. He wanted to say something significant.

'I want you to know,' his voice fumbled. 'I did not defeat Bali. Nor did he get killed by Ram's arrow. Bali gave up, by himself!'

I felt a convulsion on my skin. A lump formed in my throat. The nails of my foot dug into the soil. A few loose stones were thrown up. 'Why ...?' Words jumbled before me, as much as I tried to keep steady.

Sugreev knelt like a prisoner of war, unfolding a tragic myth.

'Between the two of us, Bali was the object. I was only his reflection. Everything was orchestrated by him. I was comfortable with that arrangement despite our inconsequential disagreements.' He broke down again, covering his face. I waited with a stone face. 'As we grew older, life became complicated. Bali understood, I didn't.' He gazed up at the sky. 'When he banished me, I felt crestfallen, orphaned. Until I met Ram.' He paused, reminiscing and allowing memories to flow. 'I cannot describe Ram to you. He is a remedial influence on troubled souls, introducing them to all their untapped potential. He is ... godly.'

Sugreev sounded unusually warm. His praise for Ram was not the melody I was interested in. I bit down on my lip hard. A drop of blood trickled from it.

'In his company, I started reviving myself. Realizing myself. You know what that means, Tara? I saw everything I was capable of. Suddenly, I was in touch with my deserving self, emerging from the timid monkey who settled for whatever came his way. I tasted freedom.' The joy in Sugreev's voice were unmissable. He was forging a bond with Ram, even though they were apart. 'I had always been reclusive about my own truth. The truth of my strength and my intelligence. That shackle was shattered. For the first time in my life, I experienced the divine confidence … my worth celebrated.'

I couldn't deny being happy for him, in spite of my grief. Sugreev was my confidant, a partner in my amateurish endeavours. I had never prepared for a night like this, when we both would feel inadequate to flatten the barriers between us.

'Tara,' he spoke without hesitation. 'All those days we spent in the forest, working on your script, I fell deeply in love with you. Those hours, fulfilling your dreams, were the best moments of my life. The way you teased the birds and eavesdropped on the conversations of the animals, understanding them and poking fun, it all seemed surreal. I watched you as if there was nothing else to watch.'

I tightened my jaws. Why was he telling me these things now? I wanted him to stop. But Sugreev did not excuse a single veil. A life full of suppressed words poured out like a turbulent river, overflowing everything that was meant to be left discreet.

'Bali asked first,' his voice dipped, 'and I couldn't bring myself to open my mouth. I married Ruma; she has been a wonderful companion. I adapted. Life wasn't lacking, but there was nothing in it for me either.'

He paused and looked up in the air at the chunk of clouds floating in the sky. Joining his hands, he prayed for forgiveness from the deceased and thanked him for the immeasurable benevolence he had received.

'I had dreamt with great delight of both brothers standing with Ram in his war against

Lanka. I thought, for once I'd make Bali proud.' His voice quivered. 'Bali had misunderstood and banished me. I requested Ram to open his eyes as he did mine. Bali wouldn't come if invited. My only option was to lure him into a duel. On the first day, Ram waited with his bow and arrow behind a bush but couldn't distinguish between us. We looked so alike.' He hiccupped and choked. 'On the second day, Ram took position again, as I had left distinguishing marks on myself. I had never anticipated that things could take such a turn.' He looked resigned, tired, aged, hopeless.

'When I and Bali were up in the air, hurling our maces at each other, Ram slipped the arrow. It pierced the invisible bubble of fallacies that Bali was trapped inside. Just like I had faced my truth in the company of Ram, Bali found his. Opaque blinds clouding his conscience were ruptured. He saw everything with utmost precision, including the sufferings he had brought upon me, for no fault of mine.'

A gentle breeze rustled the leaves. We both sat in silence, shedding tears.

'Ram did not kill Bali. He only took the blame upon himself. He will carry the burden forever as his tribute to the deceased.' Sugreev's eyes were red, the veins on his forehead swollen.

We had both lost our dearest one. We only had each other to sit with and mourn, missing the grand presence which threaded us intricately into a family.

'If Ram's arrow just broke the shield of arrogance, how did Bali die?' I took a deep breath, bracing myself for the final revelation.

'We both had taken the leap for the mace fight,' Sugreev continued. 'My complacency was broken by then. I lifted my mace, expecting Bali to retaliate with usual dominance. When Ram's arrow intervened, Bali dropped his hands in repentance, unwilling to fight any longer. But I had already raised my hands up in the air, my muscles pulsating with newfound energy. It was too late for me to retract. Bali saw the fatal blow coming. He didn't resist.'

I leant against a banana tree, Sugreev against another. I faced westwards, he northwards. I remembered Bali's pranks, of him running ahead and me chasing him. This time he had run away far beyond my capabilities to catch him by the tail and pull him back. God knows what Sugreev remembered of him.

'Tara,' Sugreev began again. 'Finish me off with that mace.' He begged, 'No one will stop you. Not even Ruma. If not as your punishment, then as my atonement. Where else will I seek liberation from this shame?' His eyes welled up. 'Angad has grown up into a fine young man. He will take care of Kishkindha. He will fulfil his poor uncle's commitment to Ram.'

I allowed some time for the tension to settle. Who knew better than me the terrible situation Sugreev was navigating?

'You have to honour your own commitment, Sugreev,' I said when he seemed calmer. 'Ram offered his friendship to you. You have debts to repay. These are not responsibilities to be passed on,' I advised. 'The remains of Bali that rest in our hearts – we will arrange them in consonance.

As a family. You, me, Ruma and Angad.'

I shifted closer to him. We wept together.

28

'Tara!'

I jolted up from the forest floor. Was it reality or a savage dream! I had ventured into the lover's corner of the forest, hoping to find something, anything, that Bali may have left behind. Since Bali had stopped visiting, the lover's corner had turned into haunted grounds. Carnivorous plants sprawled amid tall, itchy grasses. Smoke curled upwards from the smouldering woods, as the wind hummed lingering melodies. Snakes showered venom from tree trunks. Chameleons lay in wait, their scales raised menacingly on their back. Apparitions spat curses into the air.

What is beauty? Is it only a stupid delusion that temporarily camouflages inherent ugliness? My legs hurt from kneeling on the needle-like grass as I gazed at the ruins hopelessly, when my name echoed from a distance. It was the familiar voice, one that could get my blood racing.

'Bali? Bali! Is that really you?' I searched frantically in the darkness.

'No, Tara. I am Indra,' I heard. 'Bali's father. The king of Devlok.'

'You sound like Bali.' I fell back disappointed, struggling to locate the frame from which the voice emerged. There was no one to be found. 'Father! Devraj? Have you brought Bali back to me?' I asked desperately.

'Do not run hither and thither, Tara,' the voice advised. 'You will not see me or Bali. You can only listen.'

I stopped, my ankles sore, my neck stiff. 'I can hear Bali? I can speak to Bali?' I implored. 'Will he speak to me from the other world?'

'Trust the power of illusions,' Indra said calmly. 'Yes, Bali will speak to you. I will serve as the medium. Both of you will communicate through me. Treat me like a messenger, conveying Bali's thoughts to you and

delivering your messages to him, functioning as the window between the terrestrial and the celestial.'

Overcome with gratitude, I bowed my head to the ground.

I had collected many secrets in my eventful life. Nothing was as spectacular as this. With a hand, I wiped my tears. I ran my fingers over my body, smoothing my dishevelled fur and straightening my tail. Who knew if Bali was watching me?

'Bali?' I called out, looking skywards.

The ruins were crawling back on their own. Weeds fell off, filling the air with a gentle lavender scent. The venomous reptiles slithered away. Delicate blossoms sprouted from the earth. The forest floor was adorned by the flowers of drawa, champaca and karnikara. Sharp-edged weeds softened into expansive creepers. The scary apparitions retreated, replaced by kind birds chanting hymns of love.

'Tara!' his voice resonated like his touch.

'Sugreev is doing well as the king of Kishkindha,' my voice choked as I attempted to remain steady. 'You would be happy.'

'He was always capable. He just didn't know it

himself,' Bali kept it short. 'I heard you lashed out at Lakshman. Can't digest your food until you have admonished someone?' he chided.

'Me?' I protested. 'The younger prince of Ayodhya had come to admonish Sugreev when he was with Ruma, having met her after so many months,' I defended. 'The monsoon had just set in. This melodramatic male walks into our land suddenly, fuming. He accused our king of vanishing for good, instead of preparing for the war with Lanka! I told him that Sugreev was allied to Ram as a friend, not as a slave. He must learn to trust.'

Bali was laughing. 'You need to control your temper and be more diplomatic.'

I grimaced. 'After death, every sinner becomes a saint.'

He laughed again. 'If Sugreev was to fight with Ravan, shouldn't he have buckled up?'

'So we did,' I retorted immediately. 'I had sent Sugreev to Ruma. Angad and I were training the monkeys and the bears for the impending war. The force was ready.'

'How are the monkeys? Hope they are cooperating with Sugreev,' he asked unmindfully.

What a task it had been to convince the tribe! They blamed Sugreev for the death of Bali. I had to remind them of Bali's last wish. With a vengeance they picked up their maces, promising to the dead that the animal-army would never let him down. That the wish of the dead will continue to command the living!

'I have lived up to the demand you made before departing,' I mentioned solemnly, bleeding of the thorns he left, yet holding on to dear life valuing the tasks assigned by my beloved.

'After so many years he had grown up finally to fight for himself. And for others. I had to do it,' Bali reasoned. 'Forgive me, Tara.'

'I might support you, but I will never forgive.' I flared up. 'At your dwindling breath, you persuaded me to marry Sugreev!' I breathed heavily, inhaling a barrel of air before exhaling it with great force.

'What makes everyone nurture such dastardly expectations from women? Was I entitled to nothing? Not even grieving? You are heartless, Bali. You always were,' I gasped.

That noon, with Bali lying dead before us, I had walked towards Sugreev and pulled him forward, ignoring my limbs that could give way at any moment. I announced him to resume his role as the king of Kishkindha. 'Consider him my husband, along with Ruma's.' My trembling voice had echoed across the terrain. 'After Bali's demise, this is who I choose to be. I will continue as the reigning queen of Kishkindha. Sugreev will be my husband, and the king.' I shuddered then. I shuddered now.

'Tara!' Bali pleaded from somewhere. 'It is not hidden from you that you are the greatest secret of the forest.' His voice was faint – tormented and anguished. 'Kishkindha would never have accepted him as the king unless he was your husband. Did any of us have a choice?'

'How did you know?' I asked in agony, coughing and crying.

Bali smiled. 'Ram's arrow made me see that too. As long as you believed in me, I was invincible. When I disappointed you, we continued to love each other, but the marriage had collapsed.'

Bali was less barbaric when he was on earth. Post-death, he didn't bother to filter his words. Never, even in my weakest moments, had I loved anyone other than Bali. I did not care to tell him that. A ruthless truth, voiced callously, left no room for emotional disclosures.

'The forest has always been yours,' Bali spoke again. 'Kishkindha pulsates between your fingers. The trees, the animals and the birds – everyone responds to you. Without you, no king can sustain.'

Stormy winds blew in from the east. Dust from all corners swirled, littering everything in its path. Strange were the orders of nature. Nothing was allowed to settle permanently. Everything peaceful and merry was destined to be disrupted.

'How are you, Tara?' Bali suddenly asked.

I had no answer. What kind of a question was that? What difference would the answer make for him, for us? My eyes narrowed. 'How does it matter, Bali?'

The sky darkened, the rains were about to wash the terrain. Lightning cracked through the sky. The sleeping birds clung to their branches tighter, waiting to be soaked.

'When I was with you, it did not matter. Sitting in another world, it burdens me.' He sounded melodious,

perhaps intoxicated by the nectar of Devlok. 'Death was easy. Losing the privilege to live as your husband is heartbreaking.'

EPILOGUE

The Ram–Ravan war in Lanka was a devastating clash between the godly and the immoral. The monkeys were prepared for everything. It marked their first significant war. First big performance. First collective performance. First opportunity to earn recognition for their community on a wider map. Uniforms made from thick barks were stitched to protect them from sharp objects flung during the war. Slippery leaves were crafted into shields to deflect sword strikes. My father accompanied them for medical emergencies. Lali and some more women warriors joined them. Angad refused to take me along. 'The forest needs leaders too, Mother,' he reasoned. I was left with Ruma, the elders of the forest, and the children. With tight jaws, and not a single tear in any eye, we wished them well and prayed for their victory. The monkey army soon disappeared from our sight.

As autumn arrived, beds of dry leaves covered the dusty terrain. Passing birds from the south brought news of the tribe's battle in Lanka. When the birds were absent, I sought updates from Bali. Spine-chinning stories of the war were later recounted to the others stationed at Kishkindha – highlighting the bravery and intelligence of monkeys. As time progressed, the birds also brought messages of farewell from the martyrs.

When the war ended, the country was ravaged by heat waves. The forest caught fire.

The victorious soldiers returned in due course and were welcomed with gala celebrations. Casualties of the war were huge – their sacrifices deeply felt in our hearts. Only after the guests from Ayodhya departed did life in the forest return to normal. Sugreev strategized for growth; Angad took charge of the army; Ruma returned to her research; and my father tended to the injured. Jambavan still sang his tuneless songs sometimes, while dispersing seeds randomly in the forest. Anjani ma retired to a remote range of Rishyamukh Mountain, unwilling to visit this part of the terrain ever again. Uncle Kesari remained by her side.

And me?

The pishachini of the forest went back to traversing alone over the treetops and forest grounds, monitoring the conversations of plants, reptiles, insects and birds, seldom interrupting them. The seasons slithered one after the other, bringing us to yet another autumn with the turn of years.

After the cool winds plundered the land that day, twilight had just set in. Sitting idly on a tree trunk, I watched Ruma pressing the sugarcanes and palms. A soft jingle chimed amidst the tranquil of the forest. It sounded like the bells of human anklets, slowly progressing into the interiors. This couldn't be anyone we knew. Some yards away, Ruma was engrossed in her work, unperturbed by the rhythm. I slipped behind the thick leaves. There she was – a woman emerging from the rising mist. The haze played upon her face, revealing crystal eyes and covering them instantly. Her attire flew behind her, the hair long and unkempt. Something about her was heavenly. There were no ornaments on her feet; her stroll aroused a music of its own. She looked like a lost soul, searching for something. Or someone.

Quickly, I climbed down. 'Who is there?' I called out, my voice rough.

She stopped. A few grey strands of hair that had fallen over her forehead couldn't hide her voluptuous youth. 'I heard there is a forest full of the monkeys and bears, ruled by the monkey twins Bali and Sugreev,' she said, instead of answering me. 'Is this Kishkindha?'

Something inside me stirred. With eyes bursting out of my sockets, I leapt forward to stand before her. 'Were you held captive by a human? Did everyone lose access to you for a long time? Who are you?' I hoped my trembling heart wouldn't betray me!

'Ahalya,' she affirmed with a nod. 'I was turned into rock by the curse of Rishi Gautam, my husband.'

'Why?' I almost shouted. All the clues were falling into place. The only secret kept from me was on the verge of being unmasked.

'I was in love. He wanted to stop me from loving. The world takes pride in punishing lovers. Warriors are hailed as heroes, lovers are ostracized.'

I stepped ahead to hold her hand in mine. Her creamy complexion contrasted against my fur. 'Sugreev was wary of you, Bali doting.'

The tall lady smiled, leaning towards me. 'Yes, these are the two extreme reactions whenever my story is told. Most feel scared, expecting Ahalya to bring upon disasters. Very few are not convinced; they try to find Ahalya and seek answers.'

'You are a human! You cannot be Bali's lover!' I said unabashedly, tears rolling down my eyes. 'Bali, the huge monkey? Indra's son?'

I heard Ruma shouting out to the tribe from the palmyra orchard. 'Folks, I have prepared jaggery!' They all gathered on the other side to taste the new recipe. She was drowned in compliments. Ants lined up from one end of the forest to the other to lick their share of the sweet.

After a prolonged silence, Ahalya let out a deep sigh. 'I am his father's lover.'

'Bali's father? Indra? Devraj Indra?' If I was any less curious to understand everything, I would perhaps have fainted with shock.

Yes, she confirmed. I covered my mouth with both hands, stopping myself from crying out aloud. Bali was searching for a mother? And all the while, I kept feeling sad, angry, jealous and whatnot! I wished I had Bali with me once again in this life, to hold him as his only queen.

'Can I meet Bali? Where will I find him?' she gazed at the dense forest behind me. I shook my head sadly. 'Dead!' she was aghast. 'He left the world before I could show up?'

'Tell me more, Mother,' I pleaded. Somewhere in the air, I could hear Bali laughing at my plight. My husband was dead, but a little about him was still not mine. I was to possess him completely this evening. My excitement touched the solitary terrain. Pleasant breeze played with the branches, bringing down a cluster of ripe fruits. Clouds were assembling at great speed, covering the sky with multiple layers, before dispersing again. Untimely lightning fragmented the darkness with haphazard flashes of light. Fresh embryos burgeoned from discarded seeds. Drooping buds spread their petals.

'Two monkeys appeared occasionally in the trees of our hermitage, beside the river Mandakini,' Ahalya reminisced. 'One was studious, diligently listening to Gautam's preaching. Gautam didn't check who learnt from him; he just taught. Sugreev was Surya's son. His penchant for knowledge showed. The other was naughty, jumping from one branch to another, guarding me protectively all the time. I didn't pay heed then. I didn't even notice the monkeys until I became a rock.'

'Why, Mother?' I asked, sitting before her and gently pulling her onto the grass. She obliged.

'Bali was such a charming child,' she recalled

fondly. 'His humour was endearing. He would quietly repair my hut, erect my swing, burn cinnamon, turmeric and sandalwood in the corner of the hut on weary nights, only to vanish with his twin, leaving me puzzled with the mystery of it all.'

If only Bali knew about her turning into a rock! No one told him, not even Devraj Indra. I ruminated aloud.

'My curse was dispelled by Ram ...' I heard Ahalya say. My brows furrowed. Ram! Sri Ram? Sugreev's friend, Ram? 'The divine prince of Ayodhya respected my truth, without any questions, thus releasing me from the load of allegations imposed by my husband. I was touched. His compassion returned my confidence and I was liberated from Gautam's curse.'

Didn't Sugreev tell me something similar about Ram? I did not appreciate the devotion then, not that I understood it now.

'Why didn't you come earlier, Mother?' I wondered why Bali could not trace her once the curse had been lifted.

She admitted to have retreated into covert concealment. 'Once liberated, I began to withdraw from inequitable relationships enforced by earthly conventions. I disowned all that was not mine.'

Sita had also done the same. This disowning and withdrawing. She went to Mother Earth; Ahalya came searching for Bali. I looked above, hopelessly.

'During his last days, Bali suspected Sugreev knew something crucial that led to your troubles,' I recollected, smiling and tearful at the same time.

'He was right,' Ahalya agreed. 'When Gautam accused me of being unfaithful and pronounced the curse, Bali was away. Sugreev was watching. He held back that piece of information. The younger twin was overcome with fear.' The mother was narrating as if she could see things happening before her eyes. As if Bali was still alive, Sugreev was around. 'The brothers had witnessed the human cruelty of separating lovers, where sacred beauty was sullied by a horrifying inferno. Gautam's rigidity divorced from my tenderness made Bali cynical about human ethics.'

Nightfall had begun to drape the forest in darkness. The birds chirped wearily before calling it a day. 'And what of Sugreev?' I asked with an engrossing hunger, having reached the fag end of the tale.

'Sugreev could never shake off his fear,' Ahalya replied. 'He feared Gautam would also curse Bali if he knew that the elder twin was Indra's son.' She closed her eyes, as did I.

No wonder Sugreev tried to befriend the humans and assimilate with them, hoping that Bali would be spared should the truth ever become known. Bali couldn't discern the core of Sugreev's distress. He presumed that if he brought Ahalya back, Sugreev's fears would dissipate. The elder monkey harboured a secret search relentlessly, lest the sage would discover his quest and inflict arduous challenges for the woman, making it more difficult for him to locate her.

The nobility of the twins had remained under wraps throughout their lifetimes, loving each other like no one ever could. Only in myths could such love fall apart.

I led Ahalya to the lovers' corner of the forest, where the fireflies danced and lavenders bloomed. 'Here we were, between heaven and earth, celebrating bonds that transcend boundaries. I and Bali. Ahalya and Devraj. Bali and Sugreev. Ahalya and Bali.

Ahalya breathed heavily, enraptured by the fragrance. Orange flowers blossomed near her feet, swaying their pollens back and forth. Little blue birds I had never seen before fluttered in, sipping nectar from the flowers. The forest woke up to its mysteries, for the pishachini and the goddess.

The lovers' corner was Indra's cosmic reverie created for his beloved – Bali had told me the last time we visited together. The monkey had rehashed a fraction of his father's magnificence for his wife. I blushed again, just as I did then.

Mesmerized, Mother stood before me. From above the mountains and behind the lake a dense fog floated towards us. They clutched on to thin particles, forming a blanket of thick mist, enveloping us from all sides. Overwhelmed, Ahalya stretched her hand out. The mist left droplets of water on her palm. She seemed touched, bathed, indulged – immersed in a state of trance.

Leaving Mother engulfed within the mist, I beseeched for the Devraj to fulfil their incomplete love story. Without looking behind, I stepped out of the mystic haze. A soft drizzle blessed me as I perched on a ketaki. Ruma was calling out for me from somewhere. I did not answer, waiting to be found and dragged back.

Loitering between the tamal trees, Jambavan was singing again. Wretched voice – tuneless but kind. His lyrics surveyed something by the name of Sati! I strained to listen. 'Sati, the hoarder of divine secrets,' the song revered. 'She is the purest embodiment of power that unites. Sati is the eternal giver and seeker of love.' I clasped my hands around myself, hoping that Bali could feel crushed in my unyielding embrace.

These days, it rained whenever I tried to write. Weren't the rains controlled by Devraj Indra? I had to find a safe place to preserve my writing, beyond the reach of the big monkey's pranks. Despite being dead and gone, Bali was not done echoing his father's magnificence, just to trouble his wife and keep her thoughts tethered to him. A mischievous, jobless fellow! I vowed to write about the holy reunion of souls come morning, after completing the day's chores. Maybe someday, someone would read my story too!

ACKNOWLEDGEMENTS

I must begin with the readers. Thank you for the generous response to the Sati series. For connecting with me across social media platforms and expressing your delight. For raising questions and for recommending these books to other readers and communities. I am overwhelmed.

I must specifically mention the Instagram artists whose creativity captivates me. The way you photograph the book(s) on window sills and tables, adjust the light and shadow in exquisite proportions, add pearls or plants, embellish with zari or lace – they all contribute to a terrific after-story that leaves this author humbled and grateful. You guys are fabulous. I am thankful for your feedback.

I am thankful for a very unpredictable life with magical twists, when unexpected events and conversations (or the lack thereof) reinforce ancient philosophies. I use them as resources in my writing.

Thank you, Swati Soni, for combing the internet to source relevant reading materials and research documents on Bali, Sugreev, Ruma and Tara.

In the course of my journey with the Pancha Kanya, I've been immensely thankful to the Pan Macmillan India team: Isha, Rajdeep, Teesta, Elizabeth, Saburi, Pooja, Ditsha, Santosh and Vijay. I can't stop missing Dr Prasun Chatterjee, with whom this journey had begun. Big thanks to Misha for creating the wonderful jackets for the books.

I must mention the classic paintings of artist Hemen Mazumdar, which adorn the covers of the books and make them look as divine as the titular women themselves.

Many thanks to senior authors Namita Gokhale, Amish and Arundhathi Subramaniam for giving *Tara* kind endorsements and taking time out of their hectic schedules to read the manuscript.

My sincere gratitude to author-economist Bibek Debroy for his invaluable support and encouragement. He is the knowledge bank that gracefully settles many of my misunderstandings. To author friends Chitra Banerjee Divakaruni, Ashwin Sanghi, Anand Neelakantan, Saikat Majumdar, Kiran Manral, Saiswaroopa Iyer, Anuja Chandramouli, K. Hari Kumar and Utkarsh Patel – many thanks for your unwavering support and for producing excellent work from your own tables; they inspire me immensely. Saikat, thank you for the beta-reading and the lengthy conversations that have made me think more critically.

Thanks to my mother, Ratna Dasgupta, for agreeing and disagreeing with me on different subjects. Things I want to say to her but don't sometimes slide into the stories as dialogues.

My husband, Tuhin A. Sinha, never reads my manuscripts until they come back in book form (and vice versa). But during the writing stage, we share ideas and have debates, questioning each other's thoughts, ideas and ideologies. When Google fails to provide an appropriate synonym or translation, he is my go-to person.

My son, Neev Tanish – I owe him my writing career.

ALSO IN THE SATI SERIES